Short Sail

A Douglas Files Short

Nathan Birr

Published by BEACON BOOKS, LLC

Cover Images Copyright ©
mihtiander/iStock/Thinkstock

ISBN: 978-0-9981813-8-7 (sc)

www.nathanbirr.com

Also by Nathan Birr

The Douglas Files:
Overnight Delivery – Book One
Three's a Crowd – Book Two
All an Illusion – Book Three
Shot List – Book Four
Chasing the Wind – Book Five
Blood and Treasure – Book Six
One Life to Lose – Book Seven (Coming Soon!)

Black Male – Short
WinterKill – Short

Last Resort Series
Fire & Ice

God, Girls, Golf & the Gridiron
(Not Always in That Order) . . . A Love Story

All is Calm?

The Book of Levi

To the usual cast of characters who edit and proof and
serve as a sounding board for all my ideas . . .
You know who you are, and by now,
I hope you know how much I appreciate you.

Chapter One

Monday, May 5, 2008
8:47 a.m.

JACKSON DOUGLAS WAS more than an hour into his task of trying to decipher the handwritten case notes of Dick Davis when Mason Stewart whacked him on the back of the head with the morning newspaper. It was more of a love tap than a whack, and Jackson was used to it—it was how Mason greeted him every morning when he sauntered into the office. As always, Jackson glanced at the clock to see how late Mason was.

"Hey, Mace, in before noon today."

"Good one, kid," Mason said. He being all of thirty-one. "Just for that, you can type up my notes too." He slipped off the sports jacket he claimed he wore only so his wife would think he worked someplace more reputable, then proceeded to unbutton and roll up his sleeves. Same routine every day, followed by some banter and a few jabs at Jackson or one of the other underlings, then a cup of coffee and some schmoozing with his fellow associates before heading into his office and getting down to business.

"Yeah, well, I'll be translating all morning," Jackson said. "Give them to Walker. Or Donovan."

"I heard that," Donovan called from an unseen cubicle.

Mason flung his jacket into his office in the general direction of his chair, procured his cup of coffee, and returned to Jackson's cubicle. "Slow day," he said, glancing around. MTR Investigative Services employed eight full-time associates and six part-time assistants, few of whom were in. The full-timers had offices and the private investigator's licenses. They did the "real work." The part-timers were the grunts and gofers, and the

1

part-time status was a misnomer. They were just paid less and by the hour. They often did the "actual work."

"It is a Monday," Jackson said, pushing back from his keyboard.

"Monday the fifth," Mason said, understanding dawning on him. "Darling's deposition. That explains it."

Jackson nodded. "So, notes. Does this mean you're done with the Skyler case?"

"Completely. I shadowed the guy for a week, pulled every record imaginable, initiated purchases from him under a pair of aliases, and interviewed at least a dozen of his friends and former coworkers. I know him better than his mother, whom he doesn't call, by the way."

"What's the verdict?" Jackson asked.

Mason shrugged and took a long pull on his coffee. "He could sell a guy with emphysema a pack of Marlboros, and probably would try to. I found evidence of plenty of shady business, but not what our client accused. If Skyler's sleeping with his wife, he's covering his tracks." Mason shook his head. "I don't know why we took this case, anyhow. Peeping through keyholes is beneath us." He took another big gulp of coffee.

"But that's good, right?" Jackson said. "The guy fears his wife's stepping out and you can tell him she isn't."

"No, I can just tell him she isn't stepping out with Skyler like he suspected. Doesn't mean she's loyal and true, and he still doesn't get the promotion Skyler did. And now he's out a couple grand for our fee."

"I see why you guys burn out," Jackson said.

"Yeah, well . . ." Mason answered, draining his first cup of the morning. If he didn't already, he should own stock in Folgers. "You did good work running down those names and records for me, kid."

"Thanks, Mace. Just hearing those words makes all the hard work worth it."

"That settles it," Mason said, jabbing his finger at Jackson. "You definitely get the notes."

Jackson grinned. "Sorry. Dick asked first."

He left Mason to get down to his next case, or at least hassling the next assistant, and returned to Dick Davis's chicken scratch. Dick was the oldest of the associates at MTR, a real throwback to the golden era of private investigators. Everything but the trench coat and fedora, and that was just because it was usually too warm in San Diego for such a getup. No computer, no smartphone, no spelling class beyond grade school. But Dick was a former Marine, and what he lacked in modernity, he made up for with toughness, as well as keen intuition and shrewdness. It made him one of MTR's best associates. Plus he had tenure.

Dick's most recent case had been a missing person, a young woman who had disappeared without the proverbial trace. Hired by her brother, Dick had tracked her to Las Vegas, where she was found dealing blackjack at a smoky, off-strip casino and singing in a smokier, farther-off-strip lounge by night. It was a case straight out of the '70s for a P.I. straight out of the '70s, and while Jackson hated trying to interpret Dick's copious, coffee-stained notes, he sort of enjoyed the case recaps. It was like watching a '70s detective show, without the incredibly long driving scenes.

Jackson worked until 10:45 when he was obligated by the state of California to take a fifteen-minute break. All the while, he wondered why MTR didn't employ more than one secretary to do the associates' typing. But there were rumors that funds were a little low at MTR, and it was something of a source of contention, so Jackson didn't complain. His was a little menial, but as far as jobs went, not bad.

MTR was located in a strip mall along the I-8 corridor in Mission Valley, and its break room offered spectacular views of downtown San Diego, the Coronado Bridge, and Point Loma. Unfortunately, those views were on photos hung on one of four windowless walls around the room. But they served as a reminder that outside the tan walls of MTR was beautiful Southern California. It made the eight-to-five workday a little more palatable.

Jackson filled a mug with coffee and sat down at one of two round tables. A copy of the *San Diego Union-Tribune*—likely Mason's—lay on the table. Jackson thumbed through the sports section but didn't find anything he hadn't seen on *SportsCenter* the night before.

"Save me the crossword," a staccato female voice called.

"Hey, Walker," Jackson said without glancing up. He skimmed the National League standings while listening to the familiar plunk of quarters, whirring of gears, and thump-thump-thud of a bottle of Mountain Dew falling inside one of two break room vending machines. She took her drink and pulled out a chair across the table from Jackson. He looked up as she untwisted the cap and took a swig.

Aside from Jackie the middle-aged receptionist/secretary, Tori Walker was the only female at MTR. It had never been awkward because she was one of the guys, although not for looks. She was medium height, in good shape, with vivid green-brown eyes and chin-length auburn hair that never looked quite the same. Cute if not beautiful, Tori also had the instincts and the gumption to make it in the P.I. business . . . or any business, for that matter. But she was only twenty-five and still trying to figure out what she wanted in life. So she'd told Jackson over dozens of other such coffee/Dew breaks.

"You watch the game yesterday?" she asked.

"Half of it."

"Only half?"

"Second round against the Jazz?" He shrugged.

Tori took another gulp of her Mountain Dew, and Jackson remembered his coffee. As he raised his mug to his mouth, he saw an unspecified substance floating in the dark brown liquid. The dangers of a company pot. It had been five minutes and was probably cold anyhow, so he passed.

"You talk to Mason this morning?" Tori asked.

"The usual har-dee-har-har."

"He tell you about Skyler?"

"Just that he wasn't the guy."

"He didn't tell you anything else?"

Jackson shook his head. "There something to tell?"

Tori looked over her shoulder to make sure no one was coming down the hall. It was just the two of them. "Mason had Ricky hack into Skyler's laptop."

"I thought we put the kibosh on that sort of stuff," Jackson said.

"Why do you think I'm telling you this on the DL?" She ran a hand through her hair, an action that due to her tousled hairstyle had neither a positive nor a negative effect on her appearance. "Mace had me go through some of the data, hoping I'd find something to tie Skyler to Martinez's wife or prove he was tweaking his sales numbers at LoTek. I didn't find anything, but I did notice some other irregularities."

"Like what?"

"Well, the guy kept good records—really good. He had receipts for every purchase and every sale."

"He kept copies?"

"Originals. These weren't through LoTek. He was selling on the side."

"Did they know about it?"

Tori shrugged. "I don't know. But that's not the big thing. I compared some of the receipts, and he was gouging his customers."

"How so?"

"Selling them thousand-dollar computers, then delivering cheap knock-offs at a fraction of the price. He was turning profits of seventy-five to eighty percent."

Jackson whistled.

"Yeah. And that's not the worst part. Most of his customers were churches and other charitable organizations. From what I can tell, he's scammed close to a hundred thousand over the last two years."

"A hundred G's?"

Tori nodded, and Jackson whistled again.

"And you had proof of this?"

She nodded again.

Jackson sat back. He had no reason to doubt Tori's work or her interpretation of the data. It was just ironic that Skyler wasn't cheating in other areas when he was ripping off churches and charities.

"Mason said something about other shady dealings," Jackson said. "I assume that's what he was talking about?"

Tori nodded. "He said the guy was a chump, but it didn't pertain to our case."

"So he let it go?"

She took a swig of Dew. "He said his hands are tied. Our evidence is illegally obtained and thus inadmissible in court, and he doesn't think Skyler has violated his contract with LoTek, so we can't even get him in hot water with them."

Parker Hampton poked his head into the office. "You two plan on slacking all day?"

Unseen to Parker, Tori rolled her eyes. All the associates gave the assistants grief about taking their mandatory two breaks per day. Most were good-natured about it, part of the office give-and-take. Parker Hampton, the antithesis of Dick Davis—in style and skill—was annoying to nasty about it. Allegedly, he was the only person at MTR to make a pass at Tori. She'd rebuffed him by saying he wasn't her type—her being heterosexual and all—and his continual remarks were his effort at retaliation.

"Nope," Jackson said, folding the paper. "We leave that to the pros." He dumped out his coffee and rinsed the mug, smiling all the while at Parker. Then he followed Tori out of the room. "So what do you have on your plate today?" he asked.

"Rodriguez has me combing through hundreds of bank records on the Iverson case," she said. "And then once Darling gets back from his deposition, he wants to go through his testimony with me to prep for the trial." She sighed. "And it's only Monday."

"I wonder what self-employed P.I.s do without someone else to type up all their notes," Jackson said.

"Write them on burger wrappers?"

"Yeah, and stuff them in a shoebox."

"What about you—what d'you have going today?"

"Dick's notes, then Mason's, if his threats are true."

"What are you up to now, thirty, forty words a minute?"

"That's good, Walker. Just for that, I'm not sharing Mom's taco dip with you at lunch."

She stopped, turned to face him, hanging on the corner of a cubicle. "Does it bother you?"

"Does what?"

"Creeps like Skyler who get away with it?"

"Yeah," Jackson said. "I'm applying across town for a position as Judge, Jury, and Executioner."

She gave him a withering stare.

"Yes, it bothers me, Walker."

Before turning and heading to her cubicle, she nodded. "Me too."

Chapter Two

Friday, May 9
4:44 p.m.

"I DON'T KNOW, Dick," Jackson said, lowering his binoculars. He spoke into his cell phone with his other hand. "I don't think anybody's coming."

"Ah, you might as well call it a day," Dick said. "It was a long shot anyhow."

"You sure?" Jackson asked, hoping against hope that Dick wouldn't reconsider and tell him to "stick it out" a little while longer. It was, after all, just about the weekend.

"No. Just pick up the package and bring it in."

Of course. Jackson would have to run back to the office. He quickly did the math. It wouldn't put him home till six, but that was okay. His parents were having dinner with friends, and he had the house to himself. A frozen pizza in the freezer had his name on it, and there were at least two—maybe three—as of yet unwatched episodes of *Lost* on the DVR.

"Will do, Dick. See you in a little while."

Dick chuckled, which turned into a coughing fit, which nearly turned into a 9-1-1 call from Jackson. Dick survived and said, "I'm headed home, probie. I'll see you Monday."

Perfect. Dick went home to his whiskey and cigarettes, and Jackson got to be the last guy at the office on a Friday. How depressing.

First, he had to trudge through the drizzle and out onto the Ocean Beach Pier where, earlier that week, Dick had planted a USB drive inside a manila envelope in the hopes that a case would break when a suspect came for it. Jackson had the binoculars and long-range camera to get proof, as he had Wednesday afternoon and all day Thursday. A field trip was usually preferred over office work, but when that field trip involved nothing more than sitting in a car and watching for a nervous man to grab a small package from under a pier railing, it was a toss-up. Besides, it had been overcast for three straight days, and now the rains had come. Jackson couldn't wait to get home, close the blinds, and lose himself— pun intended—in some TV.

The rain intensified as Jackson retrieved the package, and he was pretty much soaked by the time he returned to his car. He turned on the heat in his 1976 Ford Granada, a gift from his Grandpa Leroy, and turned up the radio to compensate for the noise of the heater. The Dodgers were opening a weekend series in Milwaukee, and first pitch was less than fifteen minutes away.

Traffic on I-8 was a mess, and it took Jackson twice as long as it should have to reach the MTR offices in Mission Valley. By then the rain was coming down in torrents, accompanied by thunder and lightning that turned Vin Scully's broadcast into a crackling, static mess. Clutching the package under his arm, Jackson hurried inside. At first glance, all the lights were off, but then Jackson noticed one desk lamp in the assistants' cubicles. He dropped the package on Dick's desk—he was one of two associates who didn't lock his door when he left for the night—and headed over to see who was burning the five-fifteen oil.

Tori sat at her desk, her left elbow on the edge of the desk and her left hand propping up her head while she clicked and scrolled a mouse with her right. Two empty Mountain Dew bottles stood beside her desktop computer tower, and a third that was almost empty was just out of reach beside the mouse.

"You not hear the closing bell?" Jackson asked.

Tori didn't move. "No. Darling has me digging to China."

Jackson peered at her computer. "Darling's corporate espionage case involves Glorious Day Community Church? Fellowship of Saints?" He shook his head. "Who's naming churches these days, anyhow? Used to be the community and the denomination. Maybe a prominent feature if you lived by a big mountain or something. Now they're all a bunch of touchy-feely-sounds-like-a-retirement-home-for-bunnies names."

"Seriously," she said, turning her head, "that's your beef?"

Jackson rolled a chair over and straddled it. "Skyler has you flustered, huh?"

"I don't know what it is," she said. "But for some reason, I just can't get him out of my mind."

"Didn't know he was your type, Walker."

She scowled at him. "Don't you have somewhere to be? Hot date, maybe."

"Not exactly. I have to see what happens to Alex now that Karl and Rousseau are dead."

"You're a few eps behind."

"Yeah, well." He stood and tapped Tori's shoulder with the back of his hand. "Go home, Walker. It's Friday night. It can wait till Monday."

She sighed. "Yeah, I'm leaving soon. Have a good weekend, Douglas."

"You too. Don't let it eat at you," he said. "You've got to let them go."

"Yeah. See ya."

Jackson pushed out the door into the rain, scowling at the pelting drops for a second. But then he realized that steady rain was a perfect backdrop for watching *Lost*. As he got into the car, Jackson could almost taste his waiting pizza.

*　　　　　*　　　　　*

Sunday, May 11
2:41 p.m.

JACKSON SPENT Saturday helping his mom and dad with some chores around the house, then playing Xbox and watching a combination of NBA playoffs and the Dodgers-Brewers game. It was a ho-hum Saturday that left him a little bored, and also gave him plenty of time to think over his final words to Tori the day before. *"You've got to let them go."*

9

So how come every time he thought of the Skyler case he started getting angry? Skyler wasn't the first. Jackson was closing in on two years at MTR, and even as an assistant, he'd learned enough about several cases to make him smolder at the way MTR clients were abused or mistreated. But he had also learned from Dick and Mason and the other associates that sometimes there wasn't anything that could be done about it, short of going vigilante.

David and Hannah Douglas had long been members of a well-named little church in La Mesa, California, and since he had moved back to San Diego, Jackson had made it his home church again too. The sermon Sunday morning was part of a continuing series in the book of Daniel. It was very in-depth, and Jackson found his mind wandering. And his eyes. He looked at the projector displaying sermon notes on a drop-down screen behind the pulpit. He looked back at the sound booth against the back wall, programmed by at least two computers to receive signals from handheld and lapel microphones and then send them to no less than four speakers and amps up on the platform. There were also the flat screen TVs in a few of the Sunday school rooms, an old sound system in the basement, and the computers and printers and copiers in the offices. How much had the church spent on their electronics, and how much should they have spent?

After church, Hannah Douglas made her traditional Sunday dinner, and then Jackson and his dad retired to the living room to watch the Lakers game. They lost in overtime, and Jackson felt the weekend slipping down the drain.

Jackson's cell phone woke him from a very light sleep. On the couch, David was also dozing, and Jackson muted the baseball game on TV before answering his phone. "This is Jackson."

"Hey, Douglas."

"Hey, Walker."

"Sorry to bother you on a Sunday. I didn't interrupt anything, did I?"

"Well, as a matter of fact, my dad and I were seeing who could sleep more of the afternoon away, and now he's got the inside track." He sat up slightly. "What's on your mind?"

"I want to ask you something," Tori said. "You can say no, and I mean it, I won't be hurt."

"Are you asking me out, Walker?"

"Don't flatter yourself, Douglas. I haven't been able to stop thinking about Skyler. It's been with me all weekend, and—"

"You want me to go tilting at windmills with you."

"Yeah," she said. "It'd have to be after hours, and I have no idea how we'd go about it—or what we'd even go about doing, but . . . I can't let this one go, Douglas."

He sighed. "Yeah, me either. It's been nagging at me all weekend too."

"You doing anything for real today?"

Jackson looked at David, who was somewhere between deep breathing and snoring. He looked at the TV where the Dodgers trailed the Brewers 8-2. Back behind him in the dining room, Hannah was busy doing prep work for an upcoming women's event at church. No, Jackson wasn't doing anything for real, and he told Tori as much.

"You want to meet, brainstorm?" she asked.

"Sure. You got a place in mind?"

"Meet me at the pier? Bo could use a run."

Tori lived in Ocean Beach, meaning the pier in question was the same pier Jackson had scoped out for Dick for two and a half days. It also meant it was a twenty-minute drive for Jackson.

Tori seemed to read his mind. "And I'll spring for dinner."

"You got a deal, Walker. I can be there in half an hour."

Chapter Three

FRIDAY'S STORM HAD been driven onshore by a warm front that raised the temperature twenty degrees by Saturday. It had taken another day for the clouds to clear, and by Sunday afternoon, the weather in San Diego was again living up to its reputation.

Jackson listened to the final inning of a 9-4 Dodgers loss as he drove toward the ocean. Even though they were getting clocked, he still cherished every syllable uttered by the inimitable Vin Scully. His pure, perfect cadence reminded Jackson of days gone by, listening to ballgames on warm summer nights with his grandpa. Leroy now lived on a houseboat in Marina del Rey, and as Jackson drove, he determined it was about time to make a visit to L.A. to see his grandpa.

The Ocean Beach Pier was one of the longest in the country, stretching two thousand feet out into the Pacific. At its western end, it formed a T, with another five hundred combined linear feet running north and south. Built primarily so fishermen could escape the kelp and rock beds nearer to shore, it had also become a popular hangout for both locals and tourists. It had not, apparently, developed into a good place for a clandestine blind drop.

Jackson parked in a lot by the pier. Like the beach that ran north from its base, the pier was full of San Diegans happy to be rid of half a week of gloomy weather. The warm sun and the ocean breeze felt good on his face and arms, and Jackson rested on the hood of the Granada, soaking in the warmth. He thought about the reason he was there, contemplating what could be done about the racket Skyler was running and wondering what Tori would have in mind.

His musings were interrupted by a squeaking whirr, and he turned to see a red 1985 Saab 900 Turbo whip into a parking spot just down from his. It was an ugly car in Jackson's opinion, but Tori swore by it. Her dad had gotten it for her for a song when she was sixteen, and she'd put a good ninety thousand miles on it since. That was nothing, she claimed. It would run forever. Far longer than his Granada. Maybe so, but his car had class whereas hers looked like it should be chasing Jason Bourne around Europe.

Tori got out, her hair clipped back in a ponytail so short there really wasn't a tail. She wore a red tank top and faded blue jeans that were frayed at the knees. Acknowledging Jackson with a nod, she walked around to the back of the car and lifted the hatchback. As she did, a big black lab jumped out and circled around her, his tail wagging ferociously. He was getting on in years, and a few of the hairs on his nose and around his mouth were starting to turn gray. The silver and black look was apropos, as Bo was named for Oakland—then Los Angeles—Raiders running back Bo Jackson, Tori's dad's favorite athlete of all time.

Tori clipped a leash onto Bo's collar as Jackson sauntered over. Sensing something somewhere, Bo strained to run, but she held tight. Jackson knelt down in front of him. For a moment, Bo about lost his mind sniffing and trying to lick Jackson's hands and arms. Jackson reached out and scratched him behind the ears, and Bo quickly settled down with a high-pitched whimper.

"Thanks for coming," Tori said as she removed a pair of untied tennis shoes.

"You're welcome."

She tossed the shoes into the car and slammed the hatchback. "All right, Bo, let's go."

The dog led the way, with Tori holding him back so he wouldn't bound through the sunbathers into the surf. She plodded along behind him, content to step on the tattered ends of her jeans. Jackson walked beside her, beach side, and waited for her to start.

"I went through everything again," Tori said after Bo had settled in at their steady pace. "I wanted to make sure I hadn't missed something or misconstrued the facts." She looked at him. "I hadn't."

"Lay it out for me," Jackson said. "How many churches and charities are we talking?"

"I found records for nineteen different organizations, twelve or thirteen of which were churches."

"And the total was a hundred grand?"

"More like one-twenty on closer inspection. Skyler was selling everything from laptops to security systems. Like I told you the other day, he quoted them one price, then turned around and gave them equipment way below value and pocketed the difference. Markup is one thing, but this is ridiculous."

"Why Skyler? How did he get in with all these churches and charities?"

"I don't know exactly. Maybe he used his connections at LoTek. But Mason said he was slick . . . said he could sell Marlboros—"

"To a guy with emphysema. Yeah, he told me that too."

Tori shrugged.

"And you have the paper trail to prove all this?" Jackson asked.

She nodded.

"So why not go to the police or the D.A.?"

"We got it by hacking, so it's—"

"Inadmissible. All of it?"

"Mmm, pretty much most."

"Okay, what about showing them what you have and seeing if they can go after the same info legitimately?"

"I asked Mace about that," she said, tightening the leash a little as Bo spotted a game of Frisbee and wanted to butt in. "He said that was a possibility, but doubted the D.A. would buy it. Even if so, he said we didn't have solid proof of fraud—"

"I thought we had a paper trail."

"We do. But he didn't think it was enough to convict Skyler if he got a good lawyer. And even if he was convicted, Mace doubted he'd ever end up making restitution. If the D.A. gets involved, it becomes a criminal case, which more than likely means jail time. To get their money back, the various injured parties would need to join in a civil suit, which means more trial, more lawyer fees, and five gets you ten Skyler shuffles his assets or declares bankruptcy and never pays a cent." She looked his way again. "According to Mace."

"I guess he'd know." Jackson looked out at the ocean. "And MTR has no interest in going after him?"

"On whose dime?"

"The company's, I guess."

"Right. Finances are bad enough right now."

"Okay, so it's you and me, Sancho."

"You're Sancho, amigo."

"Whatever."

The beach widened, and Bo decided to explore the new, less-crowded patch of sand. It took Tori a moment to rein him in again. "I don't care if Skyler goes to jail," she said. "He ripped off good people trying to do good things. I want to get their money back."

"That's going to be hard."

"If it was easy, I wouldn't have called you, Douglas."

Jackson frowned for a moment until he realized that was actually a compliment.

"It's not just that he took their money," she said. "Most churches and non-profits don't have a lot of surplus cash floating around. Now they're left with junk equipment and no money to buy more. And he earned their trust, then betrayed it by playing on that trust to take advantage of them. He embarrassed them. I want him to feel that same thing."

Jackson kept his head down.

"I know it's a tall order. But this one's stuck in my craw."

"I'm with you on trying to get the money back," Jackson said. "It's where this bleeds into revenge that I'm a little hesitant."

"It's not personal revenge," Tori said. "This is more avenging."

"Ehhh . . ."

"And getting the money is absolutely priority one. If we happen to make him feel like his underpants just got raised on the school flagpole, that's a bonus."

Jackson mulled a little more, pondering biblical precepts on revenge and standing up for the downtrodden and where on that spectrum Tori's proposition fit. They strolled to the end of the street that had started to run parallel to the beach. A little farther ahead, the beach curved to face the outlet of the San Diego River. Tori stopped and reached down to undo Bo's leash, and as soon as he sensed his freedom, he took off running.

"Okay," Jackson said. "How do we go about this? Any bright ideas?"

Tori watched Bo race across the sand, plow into the surf, dart back out, and then repeat. "I don't know. I was hoping . . . you might have some ideas?"

"Okay, then let me play Danny Ocean for a minute. First, we need money. We aren't going to pull this off for nothing."

"I've got some in the bank. And I was hoping we'd be able to take him for a little extra to cover expenses."

"Ideally. Second, we need to decide how far we're willing to go."

"You mean am I willing to sleep with him to get his money? The answer's no."

"That's not what I meant. I would never ask you to do something like that."

"Good, because I'd deck you."

"I have no doubt. I meant, if this backfires, we could end up in some hot water. Or Skyler might figure out what we're up to and come after us."

"I don't think he's the type."

"No, but he might hire the type. Either way, we need to determine how far we're willing to push. Where the risk becomes too much."

Tori's eyes flitted across the beach, searching for Bo. She found him weaving in and out of the water along the river's edge. "What else?"

"The big one," Jackson answered. "How are we going to get a hundred and twenty thousand smackers from him?"

Tori nodded, and they moved a few paces down the beach, away from another couple who had wandered a little too close, given their conversation.

"We could steal it, plain and simple," Jackson said. "But I'm not wild about that idea, because if we fail, we spend the next twenty years in San Quentin. The authorities aren't going to care how Skyler got his cash in the first place; they'll just care that we stole it."

"So we get him to give it to us," Tori said.

Jackson made eye contact as he nodded.

"But how?" Tori exhaled, the question as much to herself as to Jackson.

"You know there's something else to consider," he said.

"What's that?"

"Do we want to bring in anyone else?"

"You think we need someone?"

"I don't know. It gives us more options as to what sort of con we can run, might give us a bigger bankroll. But it also brings another person into the loop. Another potential leak."

"It couldn't be one of the associates," Tori said.

"No."

"I don't know if I'd even trust any of the assistants. Not to rat us out, I mean."

Jackson nodded.

"What about your brother?" Tori asked. "Isn't he a cop?"

"Yeah, in L.A."

"Could we use him somehow?"

"No."

She frowned as she directed her gaze from Bo to him. "Why not?"

"Because whatever plan we come up with is going to border on being quasi-legal, at best. And Grant is so clean he squeaks when he walks."

"Even if it was to get money back for churches?"

"Even so," Jackson said.

Tori sighed. "Well, let's not force it. If we absolutely need somebody, we'll find them. But for now, I'm fine with it being just the two of us."

"Me too."

Tori whistled for Bo, and he bounded toward them, his paws covered in wet sand. He leaped up onto Tori, covering her in sand as well. She dropped back into the sand, affectionately roughhousing with Bo. When it became apparent she wasn't getting up anytime soon, Jackson sat down beside her. After another moment, she let Bo go. He nuzzled Jackson's shoes for a moment and wandered off again.

"My dad used to watch reruns of all the old P.I. shows," she said, turning to Jackson. "*Rockford, Magnum, Mannix, Simon & Simon*. I ended up watching them with him, a strange sort of father-daughter bonding." She looked out toward the ocean. Tori's dad had died when she was a senior in high school, after raising her himself for most of her childhood.

"Nothing strange about that, Walker."

Tori turned to him, and for a moment, there was vulnerability in her eyes like Jackson had only seen once before, the day she had told him whose picture was in the locket she always wore. That had been over a year ago, on a lunch break that had turned into an hour as she told him her life story and about the pain of losing her father and best friend at such a young age.

The flash was there and gone. Replaced by fire.

"I can't help wondering what Jim Rockford would do in this situation," she said. "He was always running a game on somebody."

"He got beat up a lot too," Jackson said.

"He did."

"At any rate, I think we need to know Skyler before we know how to get to him."

"I have his full dossier back at my apartment," she said. "Everything MTR has."

"You brought confidential information home from the office?" he asked in mock astonishment.

Tori smirked. "You going to turn me in?"

"Are you kidding? And end up on your bad side?"

The smirk widened, then Tori turned over her shoulder and found Bo. "Here, boy," she said, clapping. He plodded over to her, and she rewarded him with more scratching and patting. She also surreptitiously slipped his leash back on. Then she backhanded Jackson's knee.

"Come on, I promised you dinner. While I cook, you can review Skyler's file."

"You're cooking?"

Tori nodded. "That's right."

"You can cook?"

"Since I was ten. You like Mexican?"

Jackson nodded at Bo. Tori still had her hands around the dog's neck. Jackson grinned. "As long as you wash your hands first."

18

Chapter Four

TORI'S APARTMENT WAS on the second floor of an historic-looking but relatively new building in Ocean Beach, just a handful of blocks from the actual beach. Jackson had never been there, even though he and Tori had been friends for most of the time he'd worked at MTR. Theirs had been a lunchtime and break room friendship, and although they knew each other well, they had never socialized outside work.

Tori used a hose on the outside of the building to spray the sand off Bo's legs. She then kicked off her shoes and turned the hose on her blue jeans, washing off the sand. While Bo shook dry, she racked the hose.

"You're an odd one, Walker."

"This from the guy who recreated Jim Everett and Henry Ellard on his Xbox," she said as she reached down for her shoes.

"Don't forget Flipper Anderson."

"Come on."

She led him up to her apartment and, once inside, dropped to her knees and toweled Bo the rest of the way dry. "There's soda in the fridge," she said with a nod. "Chips on the counter there, some Oreos somewhere. Make yourself at home."

Tori let Bo loose, and he wandered into the kitchen and curled up in his bed, content to rest after his afternoon romp. "Oh," Tori added before she ducked into the bedroom, "and Skyler's file is on the coffee table."

Jackson strolled into the living room and picked up a framed photo from the top of a small bookshelf. A middle-aged man smiled at the camera while a teenage girl hugged him from behind. Tori and her dad.

He put the frame back, scanned a few spines on the shelves, glanced at her collection of CDs and DVDs, and then walked over to the picture window. Facing south, it offered a pretty decent view of the distant San Diego skyline.

"If you crane your neck, you can see the ocean too."

Jackson glanced back. Tori had changed into a nicer, darker pair of jeans and a black Raiders tee, her hair down. He looked back out the window, craning his neck, and indeed spotting a thin patch of blue. Whether it was ocean or sky, he couldn't tell, and didn't quibble over it.

"You have a nice place," he said, turning back around.

"But not as nice as living with Mom and Dad, right?"

Jackson grinned. "Right."

"I have an easy enchilada recipe. You like?"

"That'll be fine."

Tori nodded at the coffee table. "You look at the file?"

Jackson picked it up and sat down at one of two stools by the counter where Tori was compiling the utensils and ingredients she would need to make dinner. While she began preparing the chicken mixture to go in her enchiladas, Jackson opened the manila folder.

Charles Skyler III, who went by the moniker of Chaz, was a thirty-three-year-old graduate of UC Riverside. With a degree in Business Administration, Skyler had bounced around a handful of companies in and around Los Angeles before going to work for San Diego-based computer provider LoTek in 2002.

"LoTek?" Jackson said, frowning as he looked up at Tori. "What kind of lame name is that, anyhow?"

"It has something to do with providing low-priced technology solutions," Tori said. "I checked their website. But yeah, it kind of gives the wrong vibe."

"Maybe we could just bill them a hundred and twenty K for a better marketing campaign."

"Keep reading."

For six years, Skyler had worked in sales at LoTek, climbing the ladder to Senior Sales Broker. According to his 2007 tax return, Skyler had raked in just under ninety grand the previous year from LoTek, in addition to his private sales. He'd made another thirty thousand as a private broker, and that didn't include the price gouging that had netted him an additional one hundred twenty thousand over the previous two years.

"We could report him to the IRS," Jackson said.

"Yeah, because then the churches and charities would get their money back for sure."

Jackson spent fifteen minutes looking through the various receipts Tori had mentioned, comparing prices and double-checking her math. He came up with $118,750 in stolen money and started to smolder again. Tori had finished wrapping the chicken mixture into soft tortilla shells, then coating them with sauce and cheese. She came around to the other side of the counter and began rifling through the papers Jackson was reading.

"Thanks, Walker, that's helpful."

She batted his shoulder as she extricated a sheet of paper from near the bottom of the pile. "Here. This shows all the people Skyler ripped off, address, any financial info I could find on them, and the amount he stole."

"You don't get out much, do you?"

"I told you, this one's stuck in my craw."

"Yeah, my craw's getting a little stuffy too."

"That doesn't make any sense."

Jackson sorted the papers and found more on Skyler's bio. He was single, never married, an only child of parents who had moved to Florida. He lived in a condo in Clairemont, a northern suburb of San Diego, apparently alone. His hobbies included skiing, gambling, and according to Mason, ogling women on the beach or at the condo swimming pool. He drank, but not to excess, and had been incriminated—though not charged—back in college for an incident involving marijuana.

"Other than burning some hash, is there anything we can dig up from his past?" Jackson asked.

Tori shook her head, her hand in a bag of Tostitos. "Not that Mason found. He said he had drinks a few times, but never to the point of getting drunk. I don't think there's anything to exploit in the marijuana thing, and I doubt he impregnated anyone in college or high school. I mean, look at him and try hitting Riverside or Mission Viejo sometime. They're not going for this guy."

She had a point. Skyler was tall and thin, with sloe eyes, a hawk nose, and an unruly crop of black hair. Add a high forehead and pointy chin, and it was a pretty sure deal the coeds weren't coming onto him for looks. Money may have been a different issue if he'd had any then. Tori's notes didn't indicate how Skyler had paid for college, either on his own or with help from Daddy, and she didn't know.

"Martinez hired us because he suspected Skyler was having an affair with his wife," Jackson said. "I wonder if he's the first to be suspicious of him."

"Mason didn't turn anything up, and he tailed him for the better part of a week."

"And there's nothing at LoTek that will stick either," Jackson said.

Tori turned and began getting plates and silverware. Somewhere out of sight, Bo lapped water with what sounded like a turbo tongue. "You want to put that away while we eat?" Tori asked. "I'd hate to get enchilada sauce on my work."

Jackson began reordering all her papers and replacing them in the folder. "I have to say, it smells good."

"Why are you surprised? I cooked every night for Dad and me."

"I don't know. You just seem more like the takeout and delivery sort to me. Nothing personal."

"What about you? You the typical guy who's mastered toast and frozen pizzas but that's about it?"

"Mom taught me the basics, so I can get by."

"Yeah, well, I kind of had to learn the basics on my own."

"I don't envy you that."

"Dad and I did all right," she said. She fingered her locket. "Let me tell you something, Douglas. You get along with your folks, right?'

He nodded.

"I mean, you're twenty-five and living with them, so you must. Anyhow, cherish every moment. They go too soon."

Their eyes met for a moment, and Jackson again noticed an intensity and openness in her eyes, this time manifested in the makings of a tear that never formed. Instead, she turned and checked the enchiladas in the oven. "Just another few more minutes."

"He's a gambler," Jackson said in reference to her notes. He reached for the plates she'd stacked on the counter and set two places.

"Wow, you know where the fork goes," she said as he laid out the silverware.

"I told you, Mom taught me the basics."

"And you're still single?"

"Remarkable, isn't it?"

Tori leaned on the counter. "He's a gambler," she repeated.

"So, maybe we can prey on that somehow."

"Any ideas?"

"What's his game? Cards, dice, sports, action in general?"

"Mostly casino games, I think." She put on an oven mitt. "You want to Willie Bank him?"

"I don't think we have the bankroll for that," Jackson said. "But if we could get him into a private card game, we might be able to run the wire on him."

"We'd need more players," she said, opening the oven. She pulled out a pan of cheesy, bubbling enchiladas and set them on a trivet. "No, Bo."

The dog whimpered but sat back down.

"And he likes girls," Jackson said.

"I thought we covered this."

"I didn't suggest anything sketchy. But girls can make guys do stupid things."

"Yes, but it's such a cliché. Girl gets guy tongue-tied, then takes him for a hundred and twenty big ones?"

"It's a cliché because it works."

"Maybe, but we'll need more than that. I can't just hang on his arm in a low-cut blouse and get him to blow a small fortune playing poker with you."

"I know."

"One or two?" she asked, scooping two enchiladas onto her spatula.

"Looks like two," Jackson said, and before the words were out of his mouth, the enchiladas were on his plate. Tori served herself a pair, then got two glasses and a two-liter of, what else, Mountain Dew. She sat down and waited until Jackson took the first bite.

"Haaaaahhhhht!"

"Oh, I meant to warn you, be careful, they might be a touch warm."

Jackson gulped down some Mountain Dew.

"But really, how are they?" she asked.

"I don't know, my taste buds are still crying."

"Funny." She cut into her own, blew on the fork, and ate. "Mmm, still good."

Jackson carefully took a second bite, and he had to admit, they were tasty.

"Maybe we could sell him a fraudulent ski package," Tori said.

"I saw that he was a skier," Jackson said. "Avid?"

"Owns his own skis. And I own a board."

"You're not a blonde though."

"So?"

"Ski bunnies are blond."

"You know this from experience, Douglas?"

"Just from TV."

"Maybe so, but board bunnies are usually brunette."

"Board bunnies?"

She stuffed a bite into her mouth with a challenging glare.

"Okay, so what, you crash into him on the slopes, giggle, then share a cocoa in the lodge? Where does that get us a hundred and twenty smackers?"

"First of all, snowboarders don't giggle. And I'm just brainstorming here."

"Gretchen Bleiler's blond," Jackson said after a bite of blown-on enchilada."

"Exception to every rule."

"Hannah Teter's blond."

The challenging glare turned dirty.

"Calm down," Jackson said. "The ski-slash-board angle could be our in. I just don't know to what yet."

"Maybe I could invite him to a mountaintop game of craps."

"Now we're working offsite too," Jackson said. "And he has to be going already, unless you can entice him to the slopes, which has you back in the old clichéd seductive female role."

"Okay, so it's a longshot. Like I said, I'm just thinking out loud."

"Lindsey Jacobellis is blond."

"I'm going to punch you right in the cornea."

"So much for your hospitality badge."

"I used to pick on the Girl Scouts in my school."

"Did you steal their cookies too? Maybe we could make this a simple smash-and-grab."

"Maybe I should have called Donovan today."

"Would it help if I asked for a third enchilada?"

"A little," Tori said, rising and reaching for his plate.

"In all seriousness, they are very good."

She nodded. "Dad liked them too."

They finished eating while debating a host of other theories and ideas on how to take Skyler for over a hundred thousand dollars. None of them had staying power. When they were finished eating, Jackson offered to help with dishes, but Tori insisted she would take care of them later. So after they had cleared the counter, they retired to the living room. Jackson sat on one end of the couch, and Tori dropped down sideways in the middle, facing him. She tucked one leg under her. "Where are we?"

"Waiting for inspiration. Beyond gambling, skiing, and lusting, does Skyler have any other interests not in the file?"

"Besides making money?"

"Besides."

Tori leaned on her arm as it rested over the top of the couch. "Mason said something about Skyler pricing sailboats."

"Sailboats?"

She nodded. "Apparently Ricky found some websites when he was looking at his browser history."

"Sailboats," Jackson repeated.

"You think that's something?"

"I don't know. Maybe."

"I don't know about you, but my brain is getting fried. And I've got more work for Darling in the morning."

"That my cue to go?" Jackson asked.

"No. I just think we need a break. Let what we know ruminate."

"Sounds like my cue."

"You're welcome to hang out for a while. I have the complete *Magnum* box set."

"You think he might inspire us?"

Tori shrugged. "Might."

"Okay. I guess I could stay for one episode."

She sat up. "I'll make the popcorn."

Chapter Five

DAVID, HANNAH, JACKSON, and Grant Douglas shared an outdoor table at Joe's Crab Shack. The restaurant was built on a pier extending from the Embarcadero into the San Diego Bay, and from their table, the Douglas family had views of coming and going pleasure boats, the curving Coronado Bridge, and a brilliantly forming sunset over Naval Air Station North Island. But Jackson was accustomed to such views and was more focused on the pile of shrimp on his plate. It was, after all, his birthday.

Technically, he was still twenty-five for another five hours and change. But his brother had driven down from L.A. for the evening during a rare night off work, so the family had decided to celebrate a day early. It didn't matter to Jackson. Free seafood was free seafood.

"So how does it feel to be a third of the way dead?" David asked.

"Oh my goodness, David," Hannah scolded. "Why would you ask such a morbid thing?"

David grinned. "Average life expectancy of the American male is seventy-eight. What can I say?"

Hannah sighed with disgust. "Don't pay any attention to him, dear."

"It's okay, Mom," Jackson said, plowing into a jumbo shrimp. "One-third isn't bad from a guy who's pushing two-thirds."

"I don't know," Grant said. "The way you eat, you might be closer to a half."

Jackson looked up. "Right, because your fish is so much healthier than my shrimp."

"I'm thinking more of your multiple deep-fryings. And multiple servings."

"It's all-you-can-eat," Jackson said. "Besides, what's with this health kick?"

"I've got to be in shape," Grant said, stretching to show off his abdomen. He tapped it slightly.

"Wow, somebody left one can of a six-pack in the fridge."

Hannah sighed again. "I thought they'd stop bickering when they grew up," she said to David.

"I don't think that will happen until Jackson catches a bad shrimp or Grant a stray bullet."

"Don't say that."

"That's why I'm taking care of myself, Mom."

"Right," Jackson said. "Snapper is known to be bullet resistant."

A departing dinner cruise tooted its horn, eliciting applause and cheers from the people onboard and several waves from those on the pier. Jackson felt the first signs that he was nearing his shrimp limit, and decided to increase his intake before he hit the wall.

"How are things on the force?" David asked Grant.

"Good. Never a dull moment."

"Any exciting stories?"

"No."

"Fire your weapon yet?" Jackson asked.

"No."

"There's always tomorrow."

"Maybe we should talk about something else," Hannah said.

"TASE anybody?"

"Only in training."

"What about you, Jackson?" she asked. "Do you have any summer plans?"

"I thought I'd maybe build a deck, do some grilling, go camping a few weekends. What do you mean, Mom?"

"I think she means, are you ever going to make anything of your life?"

"Grant," Hannah warned.

"As I recall," Jackson said, pulling the tail off a shrimp, "I've had my job about four times longer than you've had yours."

"We'll see in three months."

"How is work, Son?" David asked.

"Good. I've actually got a case, so to speak."

"A case?"

Jackson nodded. He gave them a brief, sanitized version of Skyler's activity, his and Tori's ire, and their research into how to get the money that Skyler had stolen back. All three members of his family frowned.

"What?" Jackson asked.

"Your case is revenge?" Hannah asked.

"No. Vengeance, maybe. We like to think of it as justice."

"I'm sure you do," Grant said.

"Why not the police?" David asked.

"Our evidence isn't strong enough to stand up in court. At least not yet. Plus the way we obtained it, it isn't admissible."

Grant snorted.

"Calm down there, Mr. Procedural Manual, it wasn't me who gathered it. It was my boss." Jackson shrugged as he gulped down another shrimp. "Besides . . . we don't want Skyler to get punished so much as we want to get these people their money back."

"That's noble," David said, "but be very careful how you go about it. With this much money at stake, Skyler is bound to be dangerous."

"Not to mention you're going to end up committing the same crimes he did to get it back," Grant said. "The law doesn't make provision for vigilantes."

"We're not stringing up gunfighters and cattle rustlers. We're taking down a guy the law can't touch. We're the modern version of *The A-Team*."

"And who does that make you?" David asked.

"I'd like to think of myself as a cross between Hannibal and Faceman."

"More like Howling Mad," Grant said.

"Your opinion is noted, Colonel Decker."

"There's another consideration," David said. "That's the spiritual side of this. The law is one thing; God's law is another."

"You think God doesn't want this guy to pay for what He did?"

"I didn't say that. But are you God's chosen instrument of justice?"

Jackson shrugged. "If not me . . ."

David folded his hands. "I'm not saying you're wrong. I'm a law-abiding man who believes in playing by the rules and operating within the system. But I also recognize there are times when the system has limitations."

"So what happens then?"

David shrugged. "That's where it can get very hard to discern. But if you haven't done so already, I advise you to be in prayer about it."

Jackson's phone rang before he could reply. The display showed Tori's number, and he concluded he had better answer it. He and Tori had both done some research and recon over the last two days, but their personal and work schedules hadn't enabled them to talk much.

"Hey, Walker."

"Douglas. You busy?"

"Kind of."

"I can call back later."

"No, I've got a minute." He stood and smiled at his family as he walked to a place with a little more privacy. "What's up?"

"I got into Skyler's apartment today."

"You did?"

"I weighed my options all morning while listening to Darling drone on and on, and decided to risk it. I talked to the property manager at his condo and got the vibe he wasn't real big on Skyler. As in not the kind to chat him up and let him know that his sister had stopped by to get the iPod she loaned him."

"Let me guess, his flirt-with-the-lonely-single-manager sister?"

"He was married, and I didn't flirt."

"Uh-huh."

"Do you want to know what I found?"

Jackson leaned on the railing, looking down at the dark water beneath him. "Sure."

"He's definitely interested in buying a boat. He had brochures from several companies and a note to call a guy in La Jolla. I called the guy, a little fishing expedition . . . He's selling all right. Forty-foot yachts in the ballpark of a hundred-fifty K."

Jackson whistled, drawing a look from the table fifteen feet away. He turned away slightly. "So he's looking for a weekend-at-sea sailboat, not a little pond-skimmer."

"Something like that."

"Anything else?"

"Nothing that stood out to me. I definitely didn't see any signs of a female presence."

"Didn't happen to have a hundred and twenty in cash lying around, huh?"

"No. You find anything?"

"I tailed him yesterday and today. He goes to work at the same time, comes home at the same time. Very routine. Stops at Starbucks on the way in, brings his own lunch or doesn't eat."

"You talk to anyone?"

"A few coworkers on their lunches. I found the same thing as you did with the landlord—they aren't big fans of his."

"What cover did you use?"

"Brother looking for a borrowed iPod."

"Very cute."

"I told them I was a process server filing a restraining order for a disgruntled ex."

A seagull flitted overheard, cawing to beat the band.

"Where are you?" Tori asked.

"Joe's Crab Shack."

"Treating yourself for a hard day's work?"

"Dinner with the fam."

"Oh. Then I'll let you go."

"We can talk tomorrow?"

"I'm in court with Darling all day tomorrow."

"Court. Already?"

"Different case."

"Busy man."

"Yes, he is."

"Well . . . you want to meet tonight?"

"I don't want to interrupt your time with your family."

"Grant has to go back to L.A. and Mom and Dad are early birds. Say ten?"

"Okay. Where?"

"You tell me, Walker."

"My place?"

"I'll see you then."

"You like brownies?"

The twenty-odd jumbo shrimp in Jackson's stomach tried to object, but he overruled them. "Who doesn't?"

"See you at ten."

Jackson closed the phone with a grin and returned to the table, where all three members of his family were watching him with rapt attention.

"This dinner theater?" he asked, turning over his shoulder.

Grant sipped his water. Hannah fiddled with the remains of her crab legs. David smirked. "Who was that, Son?"

"Wrong number."

"Is that so?"

"Some guy looking for the Association of Mind Your Own Beeswax."

"Touchy," Grant called in a falsetto voice.

"You're all staring at me like I just had a 'you hang up, no you hang up' conversation with my New York girlfriend or something."

"You did seem to be enjoying your conversation," Hannah said.

"What can I say? I'm a jovial person."

"Sure," Grant said. "That's it."

David continued to smirk. "Break in the case?"

"As a matter of fact, sort of. We're meeting later to discuss it."

"Meeting later?" Hannah asked.

"Yes, Mom. That reminds me, can I have my curfew extended a half hour?"

"Where is this meeting?" David asked.

"Her place."

"Do you think that's wise, Sweetie?"

"We're just working, Mom. And possibly watching a few more episodes of *Magnum*. But mostly business. And brownies."

"Brownies?" Grant asked.

"Yeah. She's making brownies."

"Yeah, sounds like just business to me."

"Is she pretty?" Hannah asked.

"A goddess, Mom. Come on, you guys. She's just a coworker."

"With whom you're watching late-night TV and eating brownies," Grant said.

"Okay, a coworker who's a decent host."

"Hostess," Hannah corrected.

"Besides, I've had girlfriends before. What's the big deal?"

"It's just been a while," Hannah said.

"Really? We're having that talk now. First Dad reminds me of my pending mortality, and now you're concerned that I'm not going to give you grandchildren before my biological clock stops ticking."

"Not sure men have a biological clock, Son."

"Thank you, Dad. Look. Our meeting is just business. We're meeting at her apartment because it beats the local hippie-infested coffee joint. We are having brownies because she's a decent host*ess*—and not a bad cook, either—and because work makes us hungry. It also makes us bored, which is why we may watch some *Magnum*—and because it's awesome and addictive as crack. She is rather attractive, but we're both keeping this professional, so nothing inappropriate is going to happen, nor will I be announcing at Grant's birthday bash that I am engaged. Anything else?"

David smirked at his wife. She was unable to suppress a return smile. Grant snickered across the table.

"Yikes," Jackson said, reaching for his iced tea. He took a long drink and sat back.

"Do you at least have time to open your presents before leaving?" Hannah asked.

"Yes. We're not meeting till ten."

"The witching hour," Grant said.

"That's midnight, Ichabod."

"I suppose we'd better get going," David said, catching the eye of their waitress and signaling for her. "We've got presents to open back at home and then Jack's got a hot not-date with his 'coworker,'" he said, using finger quotes.

"That's funny. What'd you all get me, a barrel for all of these laughs?"

Their waitress stopped by. "Can I get dessert for anyone, or are you ready for your check?"

"We're ready for the check," David said.

"Yeah. Some of us are getting dessert later," Grant mumbled. Jackson found his brother's ankle with his shoe, withdrew his foot, and kicked hard enough that Grant yelped.

"Wonder which species you have to eat to be able to dodge under the table kicks, Robocop."

"I think avoiding horse's patoots might help."

Hannah hung her head. "Oh, David, where did we go wrong?"

"Somewhere between 'I do' and 'Let's do.'"

"Okay," Jackson said, pushing back from the table. "I thought it was the shrimp, but now I definitely have to throw up."

Chapter Six

10:07 p.m.

"SORRY I'M LATE," Jackson said as Tori admitted him to her apartment. She wore black sweats and a white tank top under a half-open black sweatshirt. Her hair was pulled back and clipped up. She wore no makeup, no jewelry, and no perfume that Jackson could detect. Despite it all, she was not unappealing.

"You look nice," he said.

Tori gave him an evil eye. "I've had a stressful day," she answered, closing the door behind him. "Prep with Darling, running down leads for Mason, and breaking into a condo to find an angle on a crooked salesman. I'm entitled to comfortable clothes. You smell like a fishing trawler."

"We had seafood. Hey, Bo."

The dog acknowledged him with a lifting of his head. Then he lowered it and closed his eyes again.

"So, where are my brownies?"

"Cooling." Tori nodded toward the living room. "I loaded all the photos onto my laptop. Print 'em out and, with enough tape, you could redecorate this place to look like Skyler's."

Jackson spent ten minutes viewing photos while Tori narrated. Skyler's living room, kitchen, bedroom, etcetera. She had pictures of his closet, clothes drawers, computer desk, bookshelves, as well as anything that was sitting out anywhere. She described anything that was unclear—and some things that weren't—and also recounted the duality of thrill and fear she had experienced while in Skyler's apartment.

"It's crazy," she said. "I mean, I know the guy's at work till at least five, and I know the manager knows I'm there, but it was still nerve-racking."

"I didn't know you got nervous, Walker."

"I hide it well."

"I also can't believe the property manager fell for the 'I'm his sister' ruse either."

"I may have batted my eyelashes once or twice."

"I thought as much. These the brochures?"

Tori nodded. "Both are pretty good-sized boats. A thirty-six footer and a thirty-eight footer. I don't know much about sailboats, but these look nice."

"Berths for six, full galley, shower. Shoot, why own a house?"

"I did some pricing before you got here," Tori said. "New, models like these with all the bells and whistles can go for close to two hundred grand."

"I see why Skyler is ripping off churches."

"The guy I mentioned in La Jolla is selling a similar model for one-forty-six-five."

"New?"

"Eight years old."

Jackson nodded. "So what's the difference between the three?"

"Not much. All sleep from five to six, have a full galley, same style or type of boat or whatever."

"You're a real connoisseur, Walker."

"Oh like you know anything about sailboats."

Jackson admitted he didn't with a wince.

Tori sat back against the arm of the couch. "You think this is our way in?"

"Maybe."

She got up. "You want ice cream with your brownie?"

"If you got it."

"No, I was going to run to the store quick."

Jackson grinned. "Ice cream would be great."

Tori padded into the kitchen. "So what are you thinking, we sell him a fake sailboat?"

"No. Skyler is a salesman, so he'll be wise to anything like that."

"Then what?"

"We sell him a real sailboat."

Tori stopped with the freezer door half open. She closed it, no ice cream in hand. "What?"

"We sell him a real sailboat."

She leaned on the counter. "Pull the same con he's running on his marks?"

"In a manner of speaking."

"How do we convince him a knockoff sailboat is the real thing?"

"We can't," Jackson said. "That's why we have to use the real thing."

"Okay, you're not making sense."

"Skyler is ripping off his customers by selling them a quality computer but actually giving them a junker in a quality body."

"A bait-and-switch," she said.

"Right. Unless you're a computer expert, you won't know the difference until it's too late. But sailboats aren't computers, and Skyler has done his homework. So we're going to have to show him the real thing and sell him the real thing."

"Okay, but how do we do that without having the real thing?"

"We don't."

"So we have to have a hundred-and-fifty-thousand-dollar sailboat?"

Jackson nodded. "Yes."

Tori shook her head, then proceeded to dish out brownies and ice cream, which she brought into the living room. She sat sideways on the couch, crossing her legs under her. "Now, you want to tell me how we sell Skyler a sailboat we don't have and make a profit?"

Jackson waited a moment before answering, both to savor the delicious, gooey brownie and to make Tori suffer. "We need to show Skyler a real boat. Then, because he's a salesman and not an idiot, we need to sell him a real boat. So it's simple. We get a real boat."

"Where?"

"I don't know. Does Enterprise have a marine division?"

"Rent it?"

He spooned some ice cream into his mouth. "I think they call it chartering."

"So we charter a sailboat and sell it to him as if we own it, then keep the difference?"

Jackson nodded. "Something like that."

Tori shook her head. "I don't think he's going to drop that kind of money on a boat without looking at some paperwork."

"Well, we're going to have to sell him on it."

"I would say so."

"The way I figure it, we're going to have to put down a deposit and sign for a charter. Probably even provide a credit card in case we crash into a dock or something. But if we do this right, I'm hoping we can walk away with it being Skyler's signature, credit card, and even cash."

"How? And how are we going to afford even a charter? I told you I had a little in the bank, but I was talking several hundred. We're not chartering this kind of boat for any period of time for that, are we?"

"I don't know," Jackson said, scooping another section of brownie. "But that's only part of the expenses. We'd need IDs, documents, etcetera."

She sighed.

"That's why we need to con him twice."

"What?"

"We have to get our original operating budget too."

"And how do we do that?"

"Depends how greedy Skyler is. But I have a plan for that too."

"You've been doing a lot of planning."

"Long drive over here."

Tori sighed. "Why am I getting a sick feeling in my gut?"

"Hey, this was all your idea."

"I know. But I wasn't expecting a Paul Newman-Robert Redford production."

"Only one problem I see," Jackson said.

"Only one?"

"Yeah. We're going to need a techie."

"Ricky or Jonah."

"Yeah, but we didn't really want to involve anyone else from the office."

"You know anyone else?" she asked.

Jackson thought for a minute. "No."

"You want another brownie?"

"Yes."

Tori nodded. "They're on the counter."

He stood. "You in, Walker?"

"In?"

"With this plan? We can work out the details, but I don't want to unless you're buying."

"I trust you, Douglas. If you're just spitballing, then tell me. But if you're serious and you think this will work, then let's do it."

"I've been thinking all day, actually, not just on the drive over. I have a plan, and everything we've found fits into the plan. It's just going to take some serious prep work."

She handed him her plate. "Then get us both another brownie. We'll need the energy."

Jackson smiled. "I like the way you think, Walker."

Chapter Seven

Wednesday, May 14
4:38 p.m.

JACKSON DIDN'T GO home Tuesday night. He and Tori stayed up plotting until almost two a.m. Well before that time, Jackson had called home to let his parents know he would be out late. When he left Tori's house, he found a 24-hour McDonald's, loaded up on coffee, and headed to the MTR office. He had lots of work to do.

Fortunately, his official workload was stuff he could do anytime—research and record-searching. He spent the first few hours working on his and Tori's case, then brewed the first pot of coffee and dove into MTR work. By seven-thirty when his coworkers started to straggle in, he was no less than six cups of coffee into the longest day of his life.

By his lunch break when he ran to the bank, he had to keep moving to stay awake. But he had managed to get a day's worth of MTR work done, which left him the afternoon to do more prep work on the Skyler case, including creating a website for the newly founded Joyous Hope of the Blessed Redeemer Community Church, based in Los Angeles. It took him the better part of two hours and cost $3.17 for the domain name and another $9.99 for a month of web hosting. Using a very simple, free, open-source web design program, Jackson had a functioning—albeit simple—website by midafternoon.

On his lunch break, he had also bought four burn phones, each with a hundred prepaid minutes. That was more than he would need. Tori was out all day, and he didn't want to incorporate the MTR secretary Jackie into their plan, so using his best falsetto voice, he set up a basic voicemail menu on one of the burn phones, welcoming callers to Joyous Hope of the Blessed Redeemer Community Church. Pastor Cal was on his yearly two-week missions trip to Nicaragua, but Pastor Chad was covering his calls. Jackson doubted it would be necessary, but he had to be prepared.

After covering all his bases and taking the time to make sure he didn't have any bases he wasn't aware of, Jackson got out the burn phone and dialed the number on his computer screen.

"LoTek Computer Systems, this is Angie. How may I direct your call?"

Jackson tried to imagine he was a sandal-wearing, smoothie-drinking youth pastor. "Hi. My name is Chad Summers. I'm the Associate Pastor of Youth Ministries and Child Development at Joyous Hope of the Blessed Redeemer Community Church here in Sherman Oaks. I'm wondering if I could speak to a Mr. Skyler?"

The receptionist paused for a moment, likely still processing his litany of titles. "Mr. Skyler? One moment, please."

"Thank you."

Jackson took a deep breath. He listened to a company sales pitch set to some up-tempo pop beat for thirty seconds before the line blipped. "Chaz Skyler speaking."

"Mr. Skyler, my name is Chad Summers. I'm the Associate Pastor of Youth Ministries and Child Development at Joyous Hope of the Blessed Redeemer Community Church in Sherman Oaks." He said it a little faster this time, but still in his most laid-back, sipping on a chai latte voice he could come up with. "I'm in a bit of a bind, and I'm hoping you're the man to help me."

"I'll do what I can, Mr. Summers. What kind of bind?"

"I need fifty laptops, and I need them by tomorrow night."

"You need fifty laptops by tomorrow night?"

"Yes, sir. You see, it's a rather complicated situation. Our senior pastor, Pastor Cal, is down in Nicaragua right now ministering to indigent children—orphans, outcasts, the sick and lame. We just received word that our sister church in Mexico City has a spectacular opportunity to reach the lost in that community with the good news of the gospel, and we need to take advantage of that opportunity."

"I'm not sure I see the connection," Skyler said.

"Well, you see, our sister church—the one in Mexico City—has just received permission to open a jobs clinic in the heart of the city. In addition to teaching English to the locals, church members will be instructing classes in reading, computer literacy, business administration, and a host of other skills on a variety of levels, intended to provide the citizens of Mexico City with a way to a better station in life and a way to provide for their families—all while reaching them with the love of our Blessed Redeemer."

Jackson paused for a breath, but not long enough to let Skyler get a word in. "Our sister church has the facility to host these clinics, but they lack the electronic infrastructure to do so. We have been praying for this opportunity for so long—praying for God to move the hearts of the city officials and the zoning committee and so many others in Mexico City—and the faithful here and there have been saving and having bake sales and community garage sales and car washes, and we've saved almost seventy-five thousand dollars."

Jackson paused again, just to make sure the figures were registering in Skyler's brain. Then he said, "But perhaps we haven't been as faithful as I claim, Mr. Skyler, because we haven't used the money. We've been waiting for the Mexican government and the city officials and a whole slew of bureaucrats to okay this venture, and for the longest time, doors weren't opening. We kept saving and we kept praying, but we didn't want to commit that kind of money when we didn't know if this project would ever get under way. But now we have our window and we have our money but we have no computers. If we go through traditional channels, it could take a week before we have the machines, and we have a team leaving for Mexico tomorrow night, and I would love for them to be able to take the computers with them. If they don't, I'm afraid the very same officials and bureaucrats who finally okayed this clinic will change their minds when they see we don't have the resources to carry it out. But we do have the resources—or at least, I believe we do—and I believe that you, Mr. Skyler, are an answer to prayer. Several of my colleagues in the San Diego area mentioned your name a while back—they said you came through for them, and I'm wondering if you can do the same for us."

Jackson finally stopped, on the verge of a sore throat. Skyler took a moment before responding. "Mr. Summers, I believe I can come through for you. What sort of computers are you looking for?"

"Laptops, simple, easy to use. If you have anything of a more durable nature, spill resistant, that would certainly be appreciated."

"Let me check out some specs, Mr. Summers, and get a figure over to you. What's your e-mail address?"

Whoops. That would be the base Jackson hadn't covered.

"Sure. It's pastorchad@joyoushopeoftheblessedredeemercc.org," he said, at the same time logging back into his web host to see about creating the address. He was pretty sure his domain had come with five or ten free e-mail addresses.

"Great," Skyler said. "Give me fifteen or twenty minutes, and I will get back to you. You said your budget is seventy-five thousand dollars?"

"That's right," Jackson said. "Do you think that's feasible?"

"Oh, I'm sure of it. I'll be in touch shortly."

"Thank you, Mr. Skyler. You are indeed an answer to prayer."

As soon as he ended the call, Jackson got busy. It took him five minutes to set up an e-mail address for his alias, and then he waited. It was getting late in the day, and a handful of employees at MTR had already left. But two in particular had just returned. After conversing with Darling for a few minutes, Tori stopped by Jackson's cubicle. She wore a navy blouse with a white skirt and high heels, a look Jackson hadn't seen before.

He smiled. "How was court?"

"Long."

"I like the red, white, and blue."

"Red?"

"Your hair."

"Ish. How's it going?"

"He should be getting back to me soon."

"That's encouraging. Can I see your website?"

Jackson called up a minimized window and clicked through his simple website.

"Not bad," she said. "Where'd you get the photos?"

"Various churches in and around L.A. I'm sure it's not legal."

"We long ago crossed that bridge. You need any help?"

"As a matter of fact, you feel in the mood for a little practice role play?"

"What do you have in mind?"

"I'm going to need a banker."

"A banker?"

"To sell him on the computers. I've already burned my church receptionist falsetto, so I thought you might want to try."

"You want to walk me through it?"

They spent a few minutes going over Tori's role and the story Jackson had given Skyler. While they were talking, Mason stopped by and asked what they were up to. They brushed him off and told him to go home to his wife. Then, still waiting for Skyler to call, Jackson briefed Tori on the other setup work he had done throughout the day.

"Now we just need the mark to call back," she said.

Jackson glanced at the clock. It was five after five. "He said fifteen to twenty minutes. And this is good. It's after hours."

"Let's hope so."

Jackson's e-mail blipped. He clicked to open the message from C. Skyler. It was a well-packaged ad for a laptop computer, with several images, a list of specs, and a price: $1,169. No sooner had he finished reading the e-mail than his burn phone rang.

Jackson closed his eyes, getting into character. "Joyous Hope of the Blessed Redeemer Community Church, this is Pastor Chad."

"Mr. Summers, Chaz Skyler."

"Yes, Mr. Skyler."

"I just sent you an e-mail. Did you receive it?"

"Yes, I have it right here in front of me."

"I think I've come up with a great deal for you, Mr. Summers. Let me walk you through it. What we have here is a LoTek R200 series notebook PC. What we do at LoTek is take the exact same equipment you might get from a standard manufacturer like Dell or HP but without the Dell or HP sticker. Instead, we put our LoTek seal of approval on the machine, but we don't charge you for it. So what you're getting is a machine at roughly eighty percent of what you might pay directly from a manufacturer or at your local retailer."

"I knew you were the answer to our prayers, Mr. Skyler."

"I priced several models for you, Mr. Summers, and the R230 falls somewhere in the middle. I could get you a model for as low as $885, but given your concerns about durability and so forth, I really think the R230 is the model for you. The 15.6-inch, anti-glare screen has a patented water-resistant coating. The same is also true of the keyboard, which is one solid unit, not individual keys. That means if someone spills a soda onto your machine, for example, it's not going to leak into the motherboard or the hard drive or the DVD drive. Think of it like the coating they put on furniture so if you spill your coffee or wine, it just beads instead of staining."

"We at the Joyous Hope of the Blessed Redeemer Community Church do not partake in alcoholic beverages."

"I'm sorry."

"Quite all right," he said, smiling back at a grinning Tori. "Please go on."

Skyler cleared his throat. "The R230 comes with a five hundred-gigabyte hard drive, four gigabytes of installed memory, and an AMD A4 2.5-gigahertz processor. It has a DVD player and burner, which also plays CDs, of course, along with four USB 2.0 ports, an SD card reader, HDMI and VGA ports, and standard audio ports. The six-cell lithium-ion battery has an approximately six-hour life per charge cycle, and of course, there's both an Ethernet connection and built-in wireless. It's preloaded with Windows Vista Ultimate, Service Pack 1—the best Microsoft has to offer. And all of this is in the e-mail I sent you." He took a breath. "Any questions on any of that?"

"No, it all sounds spectacular."

Jackson glanced at Tori, who simply met his gaze.

"Now the price for this unit, which comes with a power cord and a three-year warranty, comes to $1,169. That's without any accessories such as a mouse or a separate keyboard."

"Those won't be necessary," Jackson said.

"All right. Now I can get those for you by tomorrow, but it is going to include a rush fee of seventy-nine dollars per unit. Is that acceptable?"

"I think that's very reasonable," Jackson said.

"Then we're looking at a total of $1,248 per unit. At fifty units, your total comes to $62,400. And of course, as a church, I'm sure you're a 501(c)3 and thus qualify for tax-exempt status."

"Yes, sir."

"Super. All that leaves is a question of how you will be paying. Cash is, of course, always an option. So is a business check or a cashier's check."

"Well, Mr. Skyler, here is where I need to ask you one more small favor. As I believe I mentioned to you on the phone earlier, Pastor Cal—our senior pastor—is in Nicaragua at the moment, and the account at the bank requires his signature or presence before they will release the money. Is there any possible way we can still receive shipment of those computers tomorrow but pay you when Pastor Cal returns? He's due back the day after Memorial Day." Jackson paused for a split second but didn't give Skyler a chance to answer yet. "We've been trying to get a hold of him, but the phone lines in Nicaragua are bad and they just had a storm and a mudslide, and I'm afraid we just haven't been able to reach him. Like I told you, this all came about so suddenly, and—"

Jackson finally quit and allowed Skyler to interrupt him.

"I'm afraid I can't authorize shipment of the computers without at least a deposit."

"Well, I have . . . $824 in my checking account, but I don't suppose that's the type of deposit you're looking for."

"I'm afraid not," Skyler said. "Perhaps we could arrange a deal for, say . . . five of the computers now, and the rest on full payment."

"Well, I don't know . . . I'm just afraid the bureaucrats would see that as a sign that we aren't capable of running the clinic as we intend."

"I'm sorry, Mr. Summers, but I don't know what else I can do."

"What if . . . Oh, it's too late for that. I was going to say perhaps I could have you call our bank and they could verify that our account is good for the money."

"I'm not sure they would do that," Skyler said.

"I'm sure Tammy would. She's been a member here at Joyous Hope for almost a dozen—Say, I could provide you her cell number, and you could give her a call. If you explain the situation, I'm sure she could vouch for us. Would that make a difference? I just hate to miss out on this opportunity, and I'm really afraid if we don't capitalize on this chance we've been afforded, we may not get it again. To think of the people there in Mexico City—"

Tori tapped Jackson's knee to get his attention, then made a circling motion with her finger. Dial it back. He nodded.

Skyler's pause was almost twenty seconds. "Mr. Summers, I want to see this deal through. I want to see you help these people, I really do. I tell you what. You give me Tammy's number, and I will call her and see what I can do."

"Oh, Mr. Skyler, I can't tell you how much I appreciate this." Jackson gushed for another few seconds, then gave Skyler the number for a second burn phone, and Skyler promised to call him back shortly. Jackson ended the call and lowered the phone. Then he reached into the drawer for the second burn phone. He handed it to Tori. "You're up, Tammy. Now be specific but don't be mem—"

"Spare me the Rusty to Linus speech. I got it."

Jackson held up his hands. "Darling makes you cranky."

The phone in Tori's hand chirped. With a wink at Jackson, she answered it. "Tammy McReynolds."

Jackson sat back and smirked at her nasally, whiny voice. He suddenly pictured a cranky, middle-aged lady with glasses perched on the end of her nose and held in place by chains that hung down to her leopard-print blouse. It was somewhat dubious if she drew the same motivation.

"Yes, Mr. Skyler. . . . Yes, Pastor Chad said you might be calling. . . . Well, that normally would be against bank policy, but considering the case, I think I can go ahead and confirm what Pastor Chad told you. That account does contain almost seventy-five thousand dollars. . . . Yes, sir, I can. . . . Yes, sir. . . . You're welcome, Mr. Skyler. . . . Goodbye."

She disconnected the call. "He bought it."

"Great. Now you can go audition for *The Nanny II*."

"What, I couldn't have him recognize my voice, could I?"

"No. You did fine."

"So now what?"

"Go home. Take Bo for a walk. Enjoy the sunset."

"What about you? You're twitching like it's day two off heroin. When are you going home to get some sleep?"

"As soon as Skyler calls me back."

Tori stood. "Okay. I'll see you tomorrow."

Jackson nodded and watched her leave. He was the only one left in the office, and he stood and paced. It was ten minutes before Skyler called. "Mr. Summers, I spoke with Miss McReynolds, and I think I have a deal for you."

"That's great."

"If you can come up with two thousand five hundred dollars for a down payment, as well as a promissory note signed by a bank manager, I can give you fifty laptops by four o'clock tomorrow afternoon for seventy thousand dollars flat."

"Seventy thousand. That's an increase of seventy-five hundred dollars."

"Yes, it is, roughly twelve percent of what we can consider interest. You see, Mr. Summers . . ." Skyler paused and lowered his voice. "I'm going out on a bit of a limb here. Brokering this deal in such a manner necessitates me purchasing the computers from LoTek myself and then selling them to you. Now that isn't totally unusual, but it does mean that I assume something of a risk. It also means I'll be responsible for the shipping of the laptops, a fee included in that price."

Jackson silently counted to five. "Mr. Skyler, I think that's more than fair. And still within our budget."

"Then we have a deal?"

"We do."

"Good."

"I'll go to the bank first thing in the morning to get the deposit, and I can wire that to you. And I'll check with a number of our members to see if any of them know anyone in your neck of the woods who might be able to pick up the computers for us to save you some time and money. And we'll still pay the full seventy thousand."

"That works for me. I'm pushing being late for a dinner appointment. Can I call you in the morning to work out the details?"

"Absolutely."

"Great. Mr. Summers, it has been a pleasure. I'll get in touch with you tomorrow."

"Thank you, Mr. Skyler. You are proof that the Lord does indeed answer prayer."

"Good night, Mr. Summers."

Jackson lowered the phone with a grin. So far, so good.

Chapter Eight

Thursday, May 15
7:00 a.m.

JACKSON SLEPT FROM seven until seven, then headed back into work. Aside from the big Darling cases, things had slowed at MTR. Jackson had some notes to type for Dick and some basic research for Mason, but other than that, he had time to devote to the Skyler case. So did Tori, after a morning meeting with Darling. While she was otherwise occupied, Jackson made a quick run to the Western Union shop just across the parking lot and sent twenty-five hundred bucks to Chaz Skyler.

Half an hour later, Skyler called "Pastor Chad's" burn phone and announced that he had received the money. Jackson then faxed a fake promissory note to Skyler, assuring payment of the remaining $67,500 by the end of the month. Jackson had feared Skyler would have thought better of the risk after a good night's sleep, but he hoped the big order would suck him in. After all, if he followed his typical pattern, he stood to make better than fifty grand in one deal. And Skyler had given no indication that he was having second thoughts.

Early in the afternoon, Skyler called again to arrange delivery. Jackson and Tori had debated all morning how to handle receipt, not wanting to show their faces to Skyler but also not wanting to involve a third party. But Skyler gave them the solution when he provided them with the address of a warehouse in National City, south of downtown, along the bay.

"And I should have our driver meet you there?" Jackson asked.

"I actually won't be there," Skyler replied. "I handle the sales, but delivery is another matter. An associate of mine will meet your driver. Just have him or her mention my name."

After hanging up with Skyler, Jackson reported to Tori, who was taking her lunch.

"An associate at a warehouse?" she asked. "And by the docks? Did all those episodes of *Magnum* teach you nothing?"

"Don't worry," Jackson said. "I'll go."

"And put fifty laptops in your Granada. I can go in the Saab."

"Maybe we should both go." He frowned. "Will fifty laptops fit in the back of the Saab?"

"We'll see." She took a bite of her sandwich. "Any luck on a buyer?"

"A line. A community center in Bonita is looking for fifteen to twenty cheap laptops. And I have half a dozen other calls out to schools, rec centers, something called the Wilderness Boys."

Tori furrowed her brow. "Sounds like a '90s TV show."

"Yeah, starring Devon Sawa and Erik von Detten and their dads who didn't love them enough. Anyhow, I'll spend the afternoon cold-calling."

"What do the Wilderness Boys want with computers anyhow?"

"Beats me. Maybe nothing."

She sat back. "Don't you feel a little bad about selling them cheap computers?"

"No, because we're selling them cheap computers for cheap. There's no deception about what they're getting."

"I suppose."

"Anyhow, we're supposed to pick the computers up at four-thirty. Any trouble with that?"

"Nope."

"Good. Then I'm back to the phones."

Jackson spent the rest of the afternoon making calls, trying to sell cheap laptops that he was "buying" that afternoon. He also thought of the conversation with his family about the legality and morality of the con he and Tori were running. It was all very sketchy, and he kept focusing on the greater good.

A little before four, Jackson and Tori got into her Saab and headed south. The warehouse was on Cleveland Avenue, in the shadow of I-5. Skyler had directed them to pull up to an entrance on the south side where his associate would be waiting. As Tori backed the Saab toward the indicated door, there was no sign that anyone else was present.

"You think it's a setup?" Tori asked as she put the car into park.

"We're a few minutes early," Jackson said. "Did we pick names?"

Tori shook her head.

"I've been told I look like a Steve."

"Is that so?"

He nodded.

"Tara."

"Tare-uh, not Tar-uh?"

"Tare-uh."

"Because I've heard it both ways."

"Tare-uh."

"In reference to the same person, I mean."

She stared at him.

"Tare-uh," he said.

"I assume since we don't have rings, we aren't married?"

"No, but we're very much in love," Jackson said. "Chaste, joyous, hopeful love, so no sultry looks."

"I don't even have a sultry look."

"Not what Skyler's apartment manager tells me."

She punched him.

Jackson nodded toward the street where an old Ford Taurus had slowed. It turned into the entrance and parked beside the Saab. One man got out, dressed in wrinkled khakis and an untucked polo shirt with some corporate logo on the breast. It was not LoTek.

Jackson and Tori also got out.

"You with Skyler?" the man asked.

Jackson nodded. "I'm Steve, this is Tar-uh." The look Tori shot him could have been classified as sultry.

"Andrew. You're here for the laptops, right?"

Jackson nodded.

Andrew nodded too as he glanced at the Saab. Then he smiled. "Come with me."

From deep within the pockets of his pants, he retrieved a set of keys with which he opened a standard-sized door to the right of a pair of overhead doors. He turned to his left and pressed a switch, and with a clang and a hum, one of the doors began to open. As it did so, he directed them to a stack of boxes on a crate to the right. They weren't very big, just large enough to hold a laptop and a power cord.

"Fifty, right?" Andrew asked.

"That's right," Jackson said.

"I'll give you a hand. Is that the only vehicle coming?"

"Afraid so."

Andrew nodded. "Let's see what we can do."

Fifteen minutes later, they had loaded all but five of the laptops into the back of Tori's car. The other five rested on Jackson's lap as she drove away from the warehouse. "Where to first?"

"We're meeting Edith at the community center in Bonita at five-thirty," Jackson said.

"And she's buying fifteen?"

He nodded. "I sold another five to a rec center in Chula Vista, but they can't take delivery until tomorrow. And the Wilderness Boys want two."

"At two hundred a pop?"

He nodded again. "Which puts us at forty-four hundred, minus the twenty-five hundred I wired to Skyler."

"I can liquidate about five hundred of my savings, which gets us to twenty-four hundred." She bit her lip. "I'm not sure that's enough."

"I'll keep selling tomorrow and throughout the weekend," Jackson said.

"And I've got a ten o'clock with Darling, and that's all. Everything else can wait till Monday."

"Good. Then we'll set up Skyler tomorrow."

"What are we doing with the extra laptops overnight?"

Jackson smiled.

"No."

"You want Mom and Dad asking questions?"

Tori groaned.

"If you're worried about thieves, I'm sure Bo will keep you safe."

"It's not that. I'm just afraid we'll never be able to move them and I'll own them permanently."

"If we need to, we can discount to one-fifty."

"Great."

"Cheer up, Walker. Everything's going according to plan."

"That's what they always say just before things go sideways."

Chapter Nine

Friday, May 16
5:07 p.m.

FOUR NIGHTS A week, Chaz Skyler left the office promptly at five (unless he was bothered by a youth pastor from a Pentecostal church or had a "dinner appointment"—perhaps faked to get out of a conversation with said youth pastor) and went home. On Fridays, he stopped at a local watering hole for a drink or two. Same one every time, according to Mason's research, a little place in the Gaslamp Quarter that catered to young professionals.

After mulling for several days, Jackson and Tori both agreed it was the place to cast their line. The workweek would be behind Skyler, and he'd have nothing on his mind but good times and relaxation. It was the perfect opportunity to bait him. The only problem was, they disagreed on who should be the bait.

Jackson had voted for Tori.

"Because I'm a woman, right?"

"Can you think of a better reason?"

"That's going to be too obvious. I just slink up to the bar, give him a sultry smile, and ask if he'd like to buy a boat?"

"You don't have a sultry look, remember? And I was thinking you'd spill a folder of brochures or something."

"Oh, that's a real pro move."

"It's a metaphor."

"I think you should do it. A couple of guys striking a business deal over a glass of tequila."

"I don't drink."

"Take one for the team, Douglas."

"Look, I can sell him on the boat. But that's it. You can sell him on the boat and you can also flirt with him a little. Stroke the ol' male ego. Bat the ol' eyelashes."

"I'm going to bat you."

"I'm not asking you to sell your body. But a woman can sell a man better than any man ever could."

She sighed. And lost.

So at five o'clock, she showed up in a business suit ready to unwind and flirt a little. Jackson was in the back corner of the bar, where there was no chance Skyler would ever see him. Just in case, he wore glasses and a shirt and tie and had gelled his hair. Unrecognizable to his own mother.

"You all set?" Jackson asked. They had checked out—sort of—two of the earbud communication devices from MTR, enabling them to talk across the room as if they were sitting side by side.

"I don't know how I'm supposed to do this with you in my ear," Tori said.

"That's what they all say on TV, but they all manage."

"You really think he's going to come up to me?"

"I would," Jackson said.

She looked over her shoulder.

"Professional compliment, Walker. Nothing more."

Tori turned back around. She did look good in a black, knee-length skirt and matching blazer. It was now hung over the back of her barstool, showing off a sleeveless maroon blouse. She sat with her legs crossed, facing the door. If Jackson was the type to wander into a bar and hit on good-looking women looking to blow off steam after five days of nine-to-five, Tori would catch his eye. And yet, it wasn't as if she was flaunting anything.

"What if he doesn't come over? I'm not the only woman at the bar."

"I'm more worried about what if he doesn't come in at all," Jackson said.

Tori took a sip of her cosmopolitan. "This is terrible," she said, making a face. "What's in this?"

"I don't know. I don't touch the demon rum."

"So you've told me six times today."

"You know, I hope you aren't going to be this snarky with the mark."

"I wonder if these earwigs work when soaked in liquor."

"Okay, I'll shut up."

"Thank you."

The front door opened, and Jackson glanced up to see who came in. Two guys, both with rolled up sleeves and loosened ties. On their heels was Chaz Skyler, still in suit and tie. He paused for a second in the doorway, glancing over the establishment as if he owned it.

"Incoming," Jackson said.

"I see him," Tori replied, masking her mouth from Skyler with another sip of her cosmo. She avoided eye contact with Skyler, who slowly approached the bar. He took a seat two down from Tori and nodded at the bartender. While he waited for his drink, he looked around, his eyes resting on Tori just long enough to appreciate her figure. But he didn't settle, and Tori didn't acknowledge him. Instead, she dug into her purse and pulled out her phone. She glanced at the display for a moment, then sighed in disgust. Just loudly enough for Skyler to look her way, but again she didn't meet his gaze.

"Doing good," Jackson said quietly. "He knows you're there."

Tori reached into her purse again and withdrew a sheaf of papers. The top page was the start of a contract for the sale of a thirty-eight-foot Remington 3 Series R38 sailboat. The ensuing eight pages were filled with nonsense, just text to occupy them. She studied the top page for a moment, shaking her head. Then she reached for the phone and dialed her office extension.

"Hey, Jimmy. It's me."

In her ear, Jackson carried on the other half of the conversation for the sake of pace. "He's looking."

"I just got a text from Ryan. He's going with a Catalina 380."

"The dirty, lowdown, scum-sucking swine," Jackson said.

"Yes, a text. Very professional." She sighed.

"And . . . beat, beat, beat, beat . . . beat."

"I talked to him at lunch and made every pitch I could."

"Remember to say it's final," Jackson said.

"Yes, he said it was final."

"Now, mention the money."

"Our price was better," she said, raising her voice slightly. "He said something about a friend brokering the deal and loyalty or some crap like that."

"Okay," Jackson said, balancing his eyes' attention between Tori and Skyler, "now I start to panic and rant a little."

"Jimmy. Jimmy, calm down. We'll think of something."

"I've caught at least two sideways glances. Let's wrap it up."

"Yeah. I'll call you tomorrow."

"Good work, Walker."

"You too."

With a sigh, Tori closed her phone. She gulped down the majority of her cosmo and looked at the bartender. "Can I get another one of these?" She picked up the contract, looked at it once more, then tore it in half and jammed it back into her purse. Then she drained the remainder of the drink.

"Hang tight," Jackson said. "We need him to make the first move."

Tori picked up her phone and scrolled through the menu, just playing around, killing time. Then, out of the blue, she made another call.

"Okay, adlib if you want," Jackson said.

"Come on, pick up," she said a moment later. "Ugh." She clapped the phone shut and practically flung it into her open purse. "Thanks," she said to the bartender as he handed her another cosmopolitan.

Two seats down, Skyler took a sip of vodka. He slid over to the stool next to her. "I don't mean to eavesdrop, but did I hear you mention a Catalina 380?"

Tori paused just a moment before looking his way. She nodded.

"Did I also hear right that you're looking to get rid of a sailboat of your own?"

"For not eavesdropping, you heard quite a bit."

"Beautiful," Jackson whispered.

Skyler twitched. "Sorry. It just happens I'm in the market for an ocean series cruiser."

Tori paused again. "Is that so?"

Skyler nodded as he took another drink.

"You're not just trying to pick me up? Play on my frustration?"

"If I was, would I know that the Catalina 5 Series C380 is a thirty-eight-foot sailboat with a top sailing speed of six knots, a berth capable of sleeping six, with a forty horsepower diesel engine?"

Tori's hard face slowly melted into a smile. "No, probably not. Sorry, it's been a long day."

"I can appreciate that." He extended a hand. "Charles Skyler III."

She shook his hand. "That's a little pretentious," she said, finally dropping his hand. "What does your girlfriend call you?"

"No girlfriend," Skyler answered. "I go by Chaz."

"I'm Allie. It's nice to meet you."

"Tell me about your boat."

"Careful," Jackson said in her ear. "Not too many details."

"It's a 2003 Remington, still in great shape. Less than twenty hours on the engine. Interior's factory new."

"Let's hope," Jackson muttered. He hadn't wanted to specify a manufacturer since they hadn't yet found a sailboat to charter, but he doubted Tori would be able to set the hook properly if she remained too vague. And a preliminary check of several prominent sailboat charter companies in Southern California indicated that the majority of the cruiser series sailboats they rented were either Remingtons or Catalinas. For whatever reason, Jackson and Tori had opted for a Remington.

"Thirty-eight footer?" Skyler asked.

She nodded.

"You have any pictures?"

"Not on me."

"What are you asking for it?"

"One-sixty."

Skyler sucked in his breath. "That's high."

"New it goes for over two hundred," she replied. "Our would-be buyer is apparently dropping one-sixty-two-five on a 2000 Catalina C380."

Skyler finished his vodka. Holding the glass, he nodded at the bartender. "Why are you selling?"

"The economy's in the toilet, and we need to liquidate."

"You keep saying 'we.' No ring. Boyfriend?"

"Brother."

"Ah."

"Jimmy."

Skyler nodded. "Your price flexible?"

Tori closed one eye partway and let her lips part in a thin smile. "Maybe."

Another nod. "Can I see it?"

"Are you serious?"

"I told you, I'm in the market."

"Okay."

"This weekend?"

"I'll have to check with Jimmy."

"Give him a call."

Tori smiled. "You always this pushy?"

"When I want something."

She turned and reached for her phone.

"This weekend's too soon," Jackson said into her ear as she dialed.

Tori waited about fifteen seconds. "Jimmy, me again. We might have a lead on the boat after all. Give me a call." Closing the phone, she turned to Skyler. "Sorry."

"No problem," he said, reaching into his jacket pocket. He withdrew a business card and a pen. Flipping the card over, he jotted a number on the back. "My cell," he said. "When you get a hold of your brother, give me a call."

"I'll do that," she said, pocketing the card. "I should probably get going. I'm meeting a girlfriend for dinner." She pulled a wallet out of the purse.

"It's on me," Skyler said. Before she could argue, he nodded at the bartender. "Put her drinks on my tab."

Tori returned the wallet to her purse. "You didn't have to do that."

"Consider it a pledge toward a successful business deal."

"Thank you." She stood to leave, but Skyler stopped her by putting a hand on her arm.

"You have a last name, Allie?"

"I do."

Their eyes locked for a second, and he grinned first.

"Dawkins," she said, returning the smile.

Skyler removed his arm. "Enjoy your dinner, Allie Dawkins."

"I'll call you after I talk to Jimmy."

Skyler nodded.

"Don't forget your blazer, Allie Dawkins," Jackson said.

She grabbed it and sent him a withering glare, unseen by Skyler. Then, with a final goodbye, she headed for the exit. Jackson waited five minutes and made sure Skyler wasn't looking before slipping out himself.

Chapter Ten

Sunday, May 18
4:37 p.m.

"WHY DO WE always use my apartment, anyhow?"

"Because my family thinks we are or should be dating and thus would be annoying."

"They think we're dating?"

Jackson nodded. "Or should be."

"And why do they think that, Douglas?"

"Apparently I smiled when I talked to you on my birthday. So Mom would ask you all your likes and dislikes, ready to bond with a kindred spirit, and Dad would just sit there and smirk all afternoon. And if Grant happened to show up . . . It's better we're here."

Tori raised an eyebrow. "You were smiling, huh?"

"Don't start with me, Walker."

She smirked.

"How's the title coming?"

"It's coming. Legalese is such a pain. How are you faring?"

Jackson groaned.

"That good, huh?" Tori's phone rang, and she reached to grab it. "Hello?" She lowered it and mouthed the word, "Kirk."

Jackson nodded and turned his attention back to his laptop. Finding a newer model Remington thirty-eight-foot sailboat available to charter was proving difficult. He and Tori had spent the better part of Saturday calling and visiting various charter services and had planned to do more of the same Sunday afternoon. But a squall had moved in off the ocean mid-morning Sunday, and it had been raining steadily ever since. So Jackson was relegated to searching for a charter online and over the phone. He had called everyone on his first list with no success and was currently looking for additional rental companies.

Tori talked for five minutes, then closed her phone with a grin.

"You smiling because of him or me?" Jackson asked.

"Him. Kirk's in."

"Good. Now we just need a boat."

"Maybe you should try L.A.?"

Jackson frowned. "How long does it take to sail from L.A. to San Diego?"

"Skyler said the other night that the Catalina Whatever-Series could sail at six knots."

"Super. What's that in actual distances?"

"Nautical miles are real."

He shook his head. "Seriously, why do we measure distance differently over water? Does that make sense to anyone? Maybe we should come up with a completely arbitrary unit of measurement for air travel too. Maybe trains can travel in track miles or railometers or something."

"You done?"

"Yeah."

She tapped her computer. "One mile equals point-eight-six nautical miles. L.A.'s about a hundred miles, so that's eighty-six nautical miles, which is—"

"The better part of a day," Jackson said.

"Might be worth it. Renting from farther away creates distance."

"Brilliant deduction there, Nancy Drew."

"You know what I meant."

Jackson sighed. "We might have to go to L.A. I'm running out of places in San Diego."

An hour and a half and a dozen phone calls later, Jackson had a lead on a Remington 4 Series R38 from a small charter service in Dana Point, in southern Orange County, near San Juan Capistrano. It was currently booked through Wednesday, and Jackson put in a hold for the weekend under the name of Chaz Skyler. He provided the number of yet another burn phone and promised to be in touch Thursday to confirm the Friday pickup.

"Time to call Skyler?" Jackson asked.

Tori had called him Saturday morning, claiming Jimmy had found a potential buyer in L.A. and was sailing their boat up the coast to show it to him. She promised to get in touch with Skyler if the L.A. buyer wasn't interested, hoping he wouldn't find another boat in the meantime. It was a risk, but the only excuse they could think of for not meeting with him right away.

"I say we wait till tomorrow," Tori answered. "Give the L.A. buyer a day to think about it."

"And give him a day to search the market."

"Makes one less day we have to stall him on the back end."

"Your case, your call."

"We wait."

"Okay."

She slapped her thighs. "I've got the title done, except for the particulars. You want to proof it?"

"Sure."

"Then how about some dinner?"

"What's cooking tonight?"

"I thought we'd make a run for the border."

"You know that's an old slogan?"

She shrugged.

Thirty minutes later, Jackson had proofread Tori's title for the yet unrented boat. Working off examples she had found online and using MTR resources as a guide, she'd done a pretty good job. At least as far as he could tell. With the rain still pounding, they loaded Bo into Tori's Saab and headed for Taco Bell. Jackson treated, and they took their food back to the beach, where Tori parked facing the ocean.

"So tell me more about this guy Kirk," Jackson said as he bit into a chalupa. In order to sail the boat, they had both agreed they would have to give in and bring a third person into their con. Jackson had a couple possibilities in mind, but Tori had claimed she knew the ideal candidate.

"For starters, his dad's a world-class sailor. Races, I think. Anyhow, Kirk's been sailing all his life. And he's an aspiring actor."

"An actor?"

"Yeah. Studied at San Diego State. He's perfect."

"How do you know him again?"

"I met him through a friend. He's a casual acquaintance."

Jackson swallowed another bite. "Can we trust him?"

"I said he was aspiring."

"Meaning he needs a gig," Jackson said.

Tori nodded. "We pay him a decent amount, keep the details to a minimum, and I'm sure he'll jump at the chance to hone his craft while sailing ours."

"Cute. So how do we cast him? Business partner? Other brother Jimmy? Hired hand?"

"I'm thinking boyfriend."

"You'll make Skyler jealous."

"He'll want to prove himself."

Jackson mulled a moment. "That could work. So are Jimmy and the boyfriend pals, or do I disapprove?"

"I don't know," Tori said, tossing a dog treat back to Bo. "Does Kirk make you jealous?"

"Insanely."

She winked at him. "We'll figure that out. The big question is how do we get Skyler to buy the boat now?"

"Simple," Jackson said. "He's a salesman."

"We sell him on it?"

"No. We let him sell himself."

"And how do we do that?"

Jackson paused just before stuffing the remainder of his chalupa into his mouth. "Working on that."

A boom of thunder shook the Saab, and Bo sat up alertly. When he saw nothing but rain on the windshield, he settled back down.

"So what's left to do?" Tori asked.

"Mostly tech stuff," Jackson said. "More backstopping of Allie and Jimmy, backstopping for Kirk, fake IDs, the rest of the paperwork."

"And your friend can help with all of that?"

"Mitch? Yeah."

"And he's cool?"

"He's cool."

"And the lady from your church can help with the makeup?"

Jackson nodded.

"And she's cool?"

"I told her it's a prank. Which in essence it is."

It was Tori's turn to nod. "What else?"

"I've been racking my brain, trying to figure out a way where I don't have to show up as Skyler, but I've got nothing."

"Too bad this isn't *Mission: Impossible*," Tori said. "Then Barney could rig up some device that would take his signature and transmit it to DP Charters and have it replace yours."

"Barney? Simon Pegg?"

"Greg Morris. TV version."

"Ah, very old school. I don't think Peter Graves' team had that kind of technology. Disappearing ink, maybe?"

She looked at him.

"Never mind. Gets rid of my signature, but doesn't get his. Besides, it'll be my face on camera so it'll be my handsome profile they'll remember. It has to be Skyler."

Tori sighed.

"I also have computers to sell."

"Don't remind me. I can barely walk through my bedroom."

"Just don't let Bo start chewing on them."

"Okay, so what's next? I mean, besides us each having homework."

"I want to meet Kirk. Don't say it. I want to screen him, prep him. But first, we have to nail down a time with Skyler."

Tori's phone chirped, and she fumbled for it while balancing her taco. Jackson helped her out with the taco.

"I know how much I've eaten," she said. "Whoa. It's Skyler."

"You know what to say?"

"We'll find out." She pressed a button and put the phone to her ear. "Allie Dawkins. . . . Oh, hi, Chaz."

Jackson grinned. She was doing that thing all women could do, pitching her voice just a little, inflecting playfulness and flirtatiousness without saying a single thing seductive.

"We haven't heard yet," she said. "Yeah. . . . He's not due back until tomorrow afternoon sometime. . . . I don't know, I haven't talked to him yet. . . . I'll call him. . . . I'll let him know. . . . Okay, I'll call you back after I talk to Jimmy. . . . Bye."

Jackson handed back her taco and looked at her, waiting, while eating his own Cheesy Gordita Crunch.

"Skyler is very interested," she said. "He said not to let Jimmy sell the boat to the guy in L.A. until he had a chance to look at it and counter the offer."

"What's his sudden motivation?"

"He's apparently entertaining clients over Memorial Day, and would love to take them out on his new sailboat."

Jackson grinned. "This is too good to be true."

"That usually means the mark is onto you."

"Only on TV where they need a plot twist."

"You believe that?"

Jackson shrugged.

"So, Jimmy, when will you be back from L.A.?"

"I don't know. I'm thinking of staying a few days. I met a girl."

"And risk Skyler shopping elsewhere?"

"Do we know how long he's been in the market?"

Tori shook her head. "Just that he has a deadline."

Jackson shrugged. "We aren't ready yet. Besides, if we make him wait, he'll be more likely to buy on the spot. Which is what we need anyhow."

"We just have to string him along until then."

Jackson nodded and ate a few bites, thinking. Then he said, "Okay, let's do this. Call Skyler back later tonight. Say you can't get a hold of Jimmy and he's probably out blowing your cash. Sound a little flustered. Promise him you'll get a hold of him by tomorrow night when Jimmy gets back."

"Okay, then what?"

"Call him tomorrow and tell him the guy in L.A. wasn't interested."

"And he'll want to meet Tuesday."

"It's supposed to rain."

"Suppose it doesn't?"

Jackson shrugged again. "You're a business woman. Go to an expo in Kansas City for three days."

"What about you?"

"Maybe I'll stay in L.A. for a while. Or better yet, tell him I'm having a mechanical problem."

"That will really make him want to buy the boat."

"We point out a nonexistent flaw in the boat so he'll be focused on it—and will see everything is fine—and won't be looking for others."

"And he'll want you to knock off five grand."

"I'm spitballing, Walker. Just say I'm hanging out in L.A. then."

"What if he comes to you?"

"Yikes, I don't know. Let's both go to Kansas City."

"This guy isn't stupid, Douglas."

"No, but he's eager."

"But not stupid."

Jackson sighed. "I don't suppose he'd believe I'm volunteering in Nicaragua, huh?"

"I don't think so."

"I'll think of something. Tell him I'm the one going to K.C., and I won't let you sell it without me. I feel like the controlling sort of brother anyhow."

Tori sighed and had the final bite of her taco. She swallowed. "How did we end up with you calling the shots, anyhow?"

"What'd you expect? I'm the man."

Tori didn't respond at first. Which made her sudden punch to his thigh hurt even more.

Chapter Eleven

Friday, May 23
7:14 a.m.

"YOU KNOW, DUDE, for a guy about to commit fraud, you're pretty mellow."

Jackson glanced at Kirk. "Thanks, bro."

Kirk was right. And not just about Jackson being about to commit fraud. He was mellow. He'd made peace with what he was doing (whether or not God was at peace with it was a different matter) and was as confident in his plan as could be. Skyler had agreed to a Saturday afternoon meeting at Shelter Cove Marina, where their boat would then be docked. Tori had completed all the paperwork, which had been checked half a dozen times. Jackson's friend Mitch had done an excellent job on Jackson's fake ID and all of the backstopping for Jackson, Tori, and Kirk. Everything was set. Now it was time for execution.

For his part, Kirk—alias Shane Bradley—was ready. And looked the part. He was about Jackson's height, average weight, with sandy blond hair that hung in his eyes, over his ears, and onto his neck. Or at least it would have if he hadn't flicked it every fifteen seconds with little head shakes that resembled a tic or mini seizure. He wore a faded pink polo shirt, khaki shorts, and boat shoes. His neck, both wrists, and left ankle were adorned with beaded, earth-toned jewelry that had been liberated from an Inca chieftain. The only thing in question was his acting ability, which as far as Jackson could tell, was yet to be tested. Kirk and Shane were the same dude.

Tori was back in San Diego, working at MTR. Her only job for the day, other than adding the name of the boat to the title and contract once she learned it from Jackson, was to call Skyler that evening and confirm the meeting on Saturday. She was nervous, but like Jackson, prepared and ready. He hoped.

Financially, they were still in the black. All but four of the computers had been sold, a few at a discount, over the course of the week. With their savings accounts added in, Jackson and Tori had a working budget of a little under nine thousand dollars. Roughly a third of that was being swept up in a three-day charter of the sailboat. Another two grand had gone to IDs, various fees, travel, outfits, burn phones, websites, and Mitch. Travel expenses and Kirk's fee were another grand, leaving Jackson and Tori a reasonable safety net for contingencies. Or bail money and attorney fees. Jackson hoped there would be neither.

He and Kirk had taken the bus to L.A. bright and early that morning and had been hanging out at the marina near DP Charters since just after six. Jackson had spent the ride up going over the plan with Kirk to make sure he had it down and also trying to figure out what he and Tori might have missed or not thought of. He came up with nothing. The list of things they had thought of that could go wrong—that list was much larger. But if everything went according to plan, they had a real chance to pull it off.

"Sorry to keep you waiting."

Jackson looked up to see a tall blond woman walking down the dock toward them. She wore a white polo emblazoned with a DP Charters logo, khaki shorts, and boat shoes not dissimilar from Kirk's. Jackson left it up to them to figure out who was wearing the wrong gender's shoes.

"I'm Kelly. Are you Chaz?"

Jackson nodded and extended his hand. "Chaz Skyler," he said in a slightly nasally voice. He caught a sideways glance from Kirk but ignored it.

"It's nice to meet you," Kelly said. "You picked a beautiful weekend to sail."

So it seemed. The sky was clear and crisp, and although it was only a few minutes after sunrise, the air was already warm. The forecast called for abundant sunshine and cool breezes. Jackson hoped it held.

As Skyler, he replied with a narrow grin. Skyler wasn't an overly friendly guy, and Jackson wanted his portrayal to match that. If things went the way he anticipated, the real Skyler would eventually show his face at DP Charters, and they had to believe he and Jackson were the same guy. To that end, Jackson wore baggy clothes to make his slightly larger frame appear smaller. He wore risers in his custom shoes to give him an extra inch of height. Janet—a lady from church who had dappled in the film industry during/after college and who was always involved in the costumes for VBS skits, Easter dramas, and children's Christmas plays—had done a pretty good makeup job on Jackson late Thursday night. She had whitened his skin color, given him a putty tip and high bridge on his nose, and styled a wig under a baseball cap that looked at least somewhat like Skyler's unruly hair. Jackson also wore brown contact lenses and a pair of glasses to further obscure his face. Under the circumstances, it was about as well as they could do, and Kirk had confirmed that the "prosthetics" were holding up well after twelve hours. Itching was another matter.

"Well, come on in," Kelly said, unlocking a small shanty that served as the shop for DP Charters. "We just have a little paperwork, and then you can be on your way."

"Great."

She flipped on the lights and booted up a computer, asking if either Jackson or Kirk wanted coffee. They both declined.

"Okay, here we go. Mr. Skyler, I have you down for a Remington 4 Series R38, correct?"

"Correct."

"Today, tomorrow, and Sunday."

Jackson nodded.

"It is available through Monday if you'd like to have it for the full Memorial Day weekend."

"Sunday's fine."

"Okay. How will you be paying today?"

"Cash."

Kelly smiled. "Cash is good. Let me get the papers printed."

Two minutes later, the three of them were seated at a small table, and Kelly quickly walked Jackson through all the forms and liability waivers. He initialed "CS" six times and signed "Charles Skyler" three more. He had practiced the signature hundreds of times throughout the week, having seen the original on several receipts Ricky had hacked during Mason's investigation. Jackson could sign the name naturally, and it looked authentic.

Beside him, Kirk hummed nervously, and Jackson wondered how far his acting career would go.

"Okay, and here's the last form," Kelly said. "This is just a signature saying that you have your own insurance and won't be purchasing any from us. And then we'll need a copy of your insurance card."

Contingency number one.

Jackson turned to Kirk, whose humming was a trace louder. He hoped the kid could adlib. "You have the insurance card?"

Kirk blanched. "I . . . thought you had all the papers."

Jackson sighed. "How much is your insurance?"

"Oh, we can call your company, and they can give us your policy number."

Later on, Kirk would commend Jackson for keeping his cool.

"Um, I can give you my agent's number," Jackson said. "It's a small place in San Diego, and I don't think their office is open yet."

"That works," Kelly said.

Later on, Jackson would commend Kirk for his cleverness.

"I can tap into my home computer with my phone," he said. "Maybe I can access it, in case she doesn't answer."

Jackson nodded, and Kirk proceeded to send a quick text to Tori, alerting her that Kelly was about to call.

"What's the name of your insurance company?" Kelly asked from back at the computer.

"Um, Bo and Sons."

"And your agent's name?"

"Kira Small."

"Her number."

Kirk sent Jackson an almost imperceptible nod as Jackson gave Kelly one of the burn phones Tori had (hopefully) with her. As Kelly called, Jackson exchanged another glance with Kirk.

Later on, they would both commend Tori for being on the ball out of the blue early in the morning.

From their perspective in the DP shop, she handled things smoothly, satisfying Kelly. As she returned to the table so Jackson could sign the form, he and Kirk tapped fists under the table. Contingency number one resolved.

"Okay, then I just need a copy of your driver's license and your boating license."

Jackson handed them both to her with a steady hand. But this was the moment of truth. Mitch had done good work, but forged IDs were still forged IDs. If things hit the fan somewhere along the line, this was what would get Jackson in deep trouble. But for the time being, Kelly was satisfied and, after making photocopies, returned the IDs to Jackson.

"You look different with your hat," she said.

Jackson didn't know what to say, so he nodded.

"Then again, everybody looks different from their ID photos." She smiled without a trace of suspicion. "Okay, let's get you out on the water."

*   *   *

8:11 a.m.

THIRTY MINUTES later, they had cleared the marina and were headed to the open sea, and Jackson called Tori to update her.

"Nice thinking on the insurance deal," she said.

"Yeah, sorry to put you on the spot."

"Good thing Kirk texted me."

"The old boy came through," Jackson said.

"What did I tell you?"

"How're things at the office?"

"Hectic. There's a wrench in the Darling trial."

"Which one?"

"Does it matter?"

"Not really. You going to be okay?"

"Yeah. I'll be out at three and give Skyler a call. As you're leaving Kansas City."

"I should probably have a weather report, in case he asks."

"You got a name for me?"

"*The Baby J*," Jackson said.

"*The Baby J?*"

"Basketball, maybe? A baby jumper? It works for us though. 'Baby J' is what Allie called Jimmy growing up."

"Is that so?"

Jackson nodded, a terrible phone habit.

"All else went well with getting the boat?" Tori asked.

"Seemed to. My face . . ." Jackson paused, realizing he could finally wipe off Janet's makeup and fake nose. He did so as he continued. "My face is on file now, as Skyler, and Kelly saw Kirk."

"I'm due for a haircut," Kirk said as he moved from rig to jib. Or maybe it was the other way around. Jackson's sailing nomenclature still had a few holes in it.

"Kirk is due for a haircut," Jackson told Tori. "And he's wearing fake contacts too, so his eye color is off. And we never even gave his name. This place was pretty low-tech, from what I could tell."

"No cameras?"

"At the marina, yes. We stayed out of them except to walk to the boat, when it only got our backs. Nothing inside DP Charters."

"Good."

"That reminds me, I can take these stupid contacts out. It's like wearing sunglasses that itch."

"Hard life you have, too, having to sail all day."

"Yeah. I'll call you when we're off La Jolla. Describe the hang gliders to you."

"You do that."

"The dangerous part's over, Walker."

"Yeah," she said. "Now let the hard part begin."

Chapter Twelve

Saturday, May 24
4:51 p.m.

THE BABY J was moored at a rented slip at the end of the dock at Shelter Cove Marina at the north end of San Diego Bay. Jackson, Tori, and Kirk were waiting with a cooler full of sodas, lemonades, and alcoholic drinks. There were also snacks in the kitchen. And, of course, the fraudulent title and contract for *The Baby J*. On Friday, Tori had told Skyler that she and Jimmy were willing to hand over the keys, so to speak, on Saturday if Skyler was interested. Friday night, Tori brought up the idea of bashing him in the head and taking the money. He deserved it. Jackson agreed but said they didn't need to commit any more felonies.

Friday, on the journey down from Dana Point, Kirk had shown Jackson the finer points of sailing, drilling the details into his head so Jackson could talk the talk, and pitch in if necessary. Tori had been studying all week so she could talk on a level with Skyler. They had spent Friday night plotting, running lines, creating stories, and prepping for anything and everything they could think of. They were as ready as could be.

Jackson wore baggy khaki shorts and a white, button-down shirt. He'd borrowed a jungle warrior necklace from Kirk. It was showing since he'd left a few buttons open. He was, after all, a sailor. He wore tennis shoes and no socks, and a faded Dodgers baseball cap.

Tori wore a red floral sundress. They had considered having her wear something a little more revealing to play upon Skyler's sensual desires, but both were uncomfortable with it, and besides, they were past luring Skyler. Now they needed to reel him in. More important than Tori's looks—and they were quite nice in the sundress—was her ability to smooth talk Skyler, to subtly persuade him without him feeling the persuasion.

Kirk was in a polo and cut-offs, same boat shoes as the day before. He was calm and relaxed, an improvement over his debut at DP Charters. Success bred confidence, it had been said, and Kirk was proof of that.

"Do we have an abort code?" Tori asked as they waited for Skyler.

"Abort? As in jump over the side and swim back to shore?"

"I mean, the con's going south, get out, clam up."

Jackson shrugged. "I think at this point we're pretty much at sink or swim."

"Well, dive in. He's here."

Jackson followed her gaze down the dock, where the slender frame of Chaz Skyler was strolling their way. He wore chinos and loafers with a peach button-down shirt, sleeves rolled slightly. All that was missing was the sweater around the neck.

"Who's that with him?" Jackson asked.

"He didn't say anything about bringing someone."

"Date?"

Tori shrugged. "Maybe he's playing us."

"There's an encouraging thought."

The woman was as tall as Skyler, but much better built. A black tank top revealed arms like pythons, rounded shoulders, and a neck of granite. Khaki board shorts failed to disguise the muscled legs of an athlete. Her hair was dark brown, short and curved around her chin. Sunglasses blocked her eyes, and her lips were set in a firm line.

"Great," Jackson muttered to Tori just before they were in earshot, "he brings a bodyguard."

"If things turn violent, I've got Skyler."

"We'll tag team," Jackson said, stepping onto the dock. "Skyler?"

With a nod, Skyler extended his hand. "You Jimmy?"

Jackson nodded in reply. "And you know Allie."

She gave a finger wave and a smile.

"This is Renee Duxhall, my attorney," Skyler said.

"A pleasure to meet you," Renee said with a stern face that suggested it really wasn't.

Jackson extended his hand, determined not to wince afterwards. Renee's lips didn't part as they gripped hands, a brief clash of wills that ended in a draw.

"Well, come aboard," Jackson said, leading the way into the small seating area at the stern.

"*The Baby J*," Skyler said with a frown.

"Named for yours truly."

"Aren't you older than Allie?"

Jackson paused. "You did your homework."

"Not emotionally," Tori said, standing and greeting Renee. She then offered drinks, which both guests declined, followed by a quick tour of *The Baby J*.

"If you don't mind, I'd like to take care of a few business matters first," Renee said. She lifted a briefcase and tapped it threateningly.

Tori glanced at Jackson, who shrugged. "Sure."

They all sat down, while Kirk busied himself prepping for their departure.

"First of all, I'd like to see your IDs as well as the title for the boat," Renee said. "We need to verify that this is your boat and that you have a right to sell it."

Gulp.

Tori kept cool. "Right here," she said, reaching into a manila envelope. "Here's the title, license, and photocopies of both of our IDs."

Renee took them and studied them for nearly five minutes. The only sounds were gulls overhead and Kirk, ready to sail, sipping a soda. This was another moment of truth, as Jackson and Tori hadn't expected Skyler to bring his onboard counsel to analyze their forgeries. But apparently, they passed muster.

"You ready to take this baby for a spin?" Jackson asked.

"A spin?" Skyler asked.

"Sorry, did I not use the proper nautical term? Come on, dude. Take a test drive, try her out, kick the tires. What do you say?"

"As Mr. Skyler's counsel, I do have a few more questions."

Jackson sat back down.

"First of all, why are you selling your boat?"

"As I told Chaz last week," Tori said, "the economy has taken a turn for the worse, and we could use the extra cash."

"It has nothing to do with the recent struggles to sell your parents' home in Rancho Palos Verdes?"

Jackson grinned because apparently their backstopping had been successful. And because he had determined long ago that Jimmy Dawkins was a little smug and just recently that Jimmy disliked Renee Duxhall. "What's it matter why we're selling? Your boy want it or not?"

"There's no need to get contentious."

"No need to pry into our private lives, either. We've got a boat. Your boy wants it. As simple as that."

"I'm not a boy," Skyler said.

"Easy, Poindexter. Just a term. Nobody's insulting your manhood," Jackson said with a grin at Kirk.

"Perhaps this is a bad idea," Renee said to Skyler.

"Please excuse my brother," Tori said. "He's a bit of a smart aleck, and he's also impatient." She focused her attention on Skyler. "From our conversations, I gather that you are very interested in *The Baby J*, and we're very interested in selling. I'm sure we can work something out."

Skyler nodded, and Renee proceeded to the next item on her list.

"How long have you owned the boat?"

"Five years," Tori answered. "Well, our parents did. They bought it new and passed the title to us."

"Do you have the original sales slip?"

"Just the title."

Renee pursed her lips. "What's your time frame for selling?"

"You can have it now for the right price," Jackson said.

"We're as anxious to sell as Chaz is to buy," Tori said.

For the first time, Renee's lips parted in a thin, alligator smile. "That brings us to price. You're asking one hundred sixty thousand?"

Tori nodded.

"We'll offer you one hundred thousand."

"You guys want a drink before you leave?" Jackson asked.

"You're in a hurry to sell. You've already had several potential buyers renege on their deals. One hundred is a fair offer."

"Who said anything about a hurry?" Jackson asked. "From what I understand, it's your *client* who's in a hurry to have a toy to show off over the weekend. Allie and I aren't exactly scrounging for meals."

"No, but I do see that you owe almost twenty-thousand in back taxes, with rapidly accruing interest. Unless you have a pending offer on your parents' home . . ."

Jackson hid the grin this time. But Mitch had done his work well.

"Maybe we could talk money after we take it for a little . . . spin," Tori said with a sisterly but denigrating look at Jackson.

Skyler nodded, and Renee consented.

This time, Jackson put out a hand. "I have a few questions of my own."

Renee sighed. Skyler leveled an even glare.

"You got a license?" Jackson asked Renee.

She reached into her briefcase and handed him a small sheaf of papers. Cover letter, introduction, credentials, a copy of her license. Renee J. Duxhall of Duxhall & Millikan. The letterhead listed offices in Los Angeles and San Diego, and Jackson vaguely remembered seeing a commercial for the firm—it had been corny and made them seem like cheap ambulance chasers. And, as he well knew, anyone could fake impressive-looking documentation.

"You *the* Duxhall?" he asked.

"My father."

He nodded and handed the papers back to her.

"Satisfied?" she asked.

Jackson grinned. "No need to get contentious. I'm ready if our captain is."

It was the perfect segue for Tori to introduce Kirk as Shane Bradley, her boyfriend and their captain for the day. His presence would give her and Jimmy a chance to chat while they sailed, she said. Renee and Skyler were both fine with the arrangement, although Renee did give Kirk the evil eye. Her default expression.

After all the documents had been stowed again, Tori passed out life jackets. Then Jackson helped Kirk cast off, and they puttered away from the dock and out of the small harbor, around the manmade barrier island, and out into the San Diego Bay.

"Bay or ocean?" Jackson asked.

"Ocean," Skyler answered. Kirk steered almost due south, between the Naval Station on Coronado Island and Point Loma Peninsula. When he had cleared the point, he turned west, across the southwesterly breeze, and out into the open Pacific. The late afternoon sky was a cerulean blue, cloudless and so close it was almost touchable. The ocean was calm, its swells gentle. And the sun was brilliant and warm, accompanied by a gentle, pleasant breeze. If not for the con underway, it would have been a perfect way to spend a Saturday afternoon.

While Kirk handled the sailing duties, turning north along the coast, Tori passed out hors d'oeuvres, then chatted with Skyler, trying to loosen him up. She interweaved stories about her and Jimmy's sailing adventures with their parents along with details about the boat and its features and specs. He was buying it, or at the very least, not hostile. Ideally, Jackson should have been working on Renee, trying to butter her up. But ideally, she should also look more like Charlize Theron and less like a starting forward for the Clippers.

After cruising north for a mile or two, Kirk turned *The Baby J* around and offered Skyler a chance at the helm. It took him a few minutes to get comfortable, but he was able to handle the boat by himself, doing so with a smirk that was part pleasure and part dreaming about showing off to his clients on Monday. If Jackson was reading him right.

Tori retrieved a bottle of lemonade from the cooler and again offered drinks and more snacks. Renee accepted a non-alcoholic beverage while Skyler opted for a beer. At the wheel, he tacked west, farther into the ocean, then south past the entrance to the bay. Satisfied with the boat's handling, he turned control back to Kirk and allowed Tori to show him around the interior. Kirk, meanwhile, circled around and then trimmed the sail, allowing them to coast on the swells for a while.

"Another beer?" Jackson asked Skyler. "Renee?"

Skyler accepted. She stood pat. "You don't drink?" she asked.

"Dad had a problem with alcohol, so I've stayed clear."

"Admirable."

"My middle name." He did retrieve a bottle of lemonade and twisted the cap off it. "So, what do you think, Charlie?"

Skyler glanced at him and took a swig of his second beer.

Jackson pushed it. "You want to talk realistic terms?"

"One-sixty is way too high," Renee said for him.

"And one hundred even is way too low." Jackson nodded at Skyler again. "Are you interested?"

He glanced at Renee.

"Come on, dude," Jackson said. "This isn't some secret society. We know you want it. You know we want to sell it. Let's put our cards on the table."

Skyler set down his beer. "Yeah, I'm interested."

"Good. Then let's talk numbers. We can drop to one-fifty."

Renee snorted. "One-ten."

Jackson laughed. "Let's cut to the chase. One-thirty."

"One-fifteen."

"I meant one-thirty's in the middle. Can we agree on that?"

"One-twenty."

"One-thirty." He grinned. "This sounds like Bugs and Daffy."

Renee paused a moment. "Let me talk to my client."

Jackson shook his head with another laugh. "You want us to go for a quick swim or something?"

"We'll be below deck," Tori said, pulling Jackson's arm.

Kirk joined them, and they closed the hatch door behind them. Tori asked the question with her eyes.

Jackson made a reeling motion with his hands.

"You think so?" Kirk whispered.

"If we can get Renee out of the way."

"Maybe we could dump her overboard," Tori said.

"It's a thought, but it'd take at least two of us."

She grinned slyly.

"Anything else we can do to sell him?" Kirk asked.

"Well, she should probably give you a kiss or two."

"What?" Tori asked.

"He is your boyfriend. A little PDA would go a long ways."

Kirk shrugged. "Fine with me."

Tori gave Jackson an evil eye.

"You're the one who cast him as your boyfriend."

"You did?" Kirk asked.

"Will you stop it?" Tori hissed at Jackson.

A knock sounded on the door.

"Don't worry," Kirk said. "I'll be a gentleman."

Tori rolled her eyes.

"In character, Walker."

Jackson opened the door and found Skyler waiting. They all took seats, even Kirk.

"My client is prepared to offer one hundred twenty-five thousand," Renee said evenly. "No more."

Jackson looked at Tori. Subtracting the one-eighteen and change that went to reimburse the various churches and charities, that netted them just over six grand, which would more than cover the money from their savings accounts they had used to finance the con—which was also approximately the amount they had left in their "contingency fund." In other words, they would net just over six grand. But Jackson had to make them earn it.

"That's a little low," he said. "We're selling for one-sixty, you lowball us, and then compromise closer to your number."

"The market is much higher," Tori said.

"We don't care about the market," Renee said. "It's a matter of what you can get from Mr. Skyler right here and now."

"I can always charter a boat for the weekend and buy at my leisure," he said.

Jackson looked at Tori again. Then he turned to Skyler. "I'm surprised. I got the feeling you were a power broker."

"You think I'm not?"

"I'm just surprised you're letting her handle all the negotiations."

"Do we have a deal or not?" Renee sighed.

"Give us a minute," Jackson said, and he and Tori withdrew into the berth again.

"It covers expenses," she said.

"More than."

"You were hoping for more?"

"No, that would be unethical."

"So we accept?"

Jackson nodded.

She reached a hand to stop him from leaving. "Is it really this easy?"

"I guess so. Ready?"

Tori nodded, and Jackson opened the door. He stopped cold. Renee held a pistol, aimed at Kirk's chest.

Chapter Thirteen

6:21 p.m.

"ONE-TWENTY?" JACKSON asked. "We're flexible."

"Shut up."

He glanced at Tori, who so far was keeping her cool. Kirk, on the other hand, looked ready to panic.

"You want to tell me what's going on?" Jackson asked.

"I was going to ask you the same thing," Renee said.

Jackson held out his hands. "Why? What's the matter?"

"He is not Shane Bradley."

"How'd you know?"

Tori hit Jackson.

"Might as well tell them, Al." He turned his eye to Renee, who didn't respond. Meaning she still bought his and Tori's aliases or that she was even cooler than they were.

"Because I know his name is Kirk Taylor. His father plays tennis with my uncle."

That explained the look she had given Kirk when Tori had introduced him.

"And you want to shoot him because of that?" Jackson asked.

"No, I want to shoot you because of that."

"Kirk's old man beat your uncle, I take it?"

"You've got a lot of lip."

Jackson shook his head. "You're making a big deal out of nothing. We brought Kirk in because neither of us can sail a boat."

"What?"

"Why do you think we're selling? This was Dad's boat, willed to us. We don't want the stupid thing or the taxes."

"You said you sailed to L.A. last weekend," Skyler said.

"Kirk and me, yeah."

Renee shook her head. "Why the alias?"

"We had to explain his presence somehow," Tori said when Jackson faltered for a moment. "Saying we couldn't sail is embarrassing, and we thought if you thought he was my boyfriend . . . it would be less awkward."

"So why not claim Kirk was your boyfriend? Why change the name? What's going on?"

"Do your uncle and Kirk's old man talk during tennis?" Jackson asked. "Because if they did, you'd know Kirk took acting lessons at San Diego State. He was doing a character. That's the only reason he's involved at all."

Renee glanced at Skyler. She still hadn't lowered the gun.

"Why should I believe anything you've told us?"

"Because you did your homework. You know about our parents, their house, our taxes. You think we're running some big con on you? To sell a boat? What's our angle?"

"I don't know. And I don't care. This deal's over."

"Wait," Tori said, looking at Skyler. "We made a mistake. We thought you wouldn't want to buy from us if we didn't know anything about sailboats. So we brought Kirk in. We should have leveled with you. But that doesn't change the facts. We have a boat you want. We can still make this work."

"I strongly advise you to walk away," Renee said.

"You won't get an offer like this. You know this boat's worth a hundred and fifty thousand. And you have a chance to get it for one-twenty-five. Don't blow it."

Skyler was clearly thinking.

"Charles, you brought me here to advise you. You're paying me good money for my advice, so I suggest you take it."

"You have to ask yourself," Jackson said, "how good of advice is it to tell you to turn away from this deal because she says so? She put on your pants for you in the morning too?"

"Shut up," Renee said.

"What are you going to do, shoot me and hire your dad to defend you?"

She stared at him but lowered the gun.

"Why do you have a gun anyhow?" Tori asked.

"Self-defense."

"You expecting to get mugged by an orca?" Jackson asked.

"You think all I have in this briefcase are my papers and a notepad?"

"You brought the cash?"

She raised the gun again.

"I'm not going to steal it from you," Jackson said with a forced laugh. "What do you think I am?"

"I have no idea. Other than a liar."

"Look, we apologized for that," Tori said. "Please. We can still make this work."

"Why?" Skyler said with a sneer. "Why should I go through with it?"

"Because you aren't going to find a better deal," she said. "We both want this. We lied to you; you pulled a gun on us. Let's call it even and make this deal."

"Forget the lawyer," Jackson said. "Ask yourself what makes sense."

Skyler clearly was deliberating again. Jackson opened his mouth to push some more but decided not to overdo it. Skyler was a bottom line sort of guy. And the bottom line said to buy. Plus, with any luck, he was thinking of the $67,500 he expected at the end of the month from Pastor Chad at Joyous Hope of Our Blessed Redeemer Community Church.

"Give us a minute," Skyler said.

"You're not going to pull a gun when we come out, are you?" Jackson asked.

Renee gave him an evil glare but put the gun away.

Jackson, Tori, and Kirk once again withdrew to the berth.

"You all right?" Jackson asked Kirk.

"I am now."

Jackson gave him a reassuring pat on the shoulder.

"Did we blow it?" Tori asked.

Jackson held up his thumb and index finger. "This close. But your suggestion at having an abort code was spot on."

"That was quick thinking," Kirk said. "Who knew Dad played tennis with her uncle?"

"Not you, apparently."

"I'm still wondering what kind of lawyer packs a gun," Tori said. "In San Diego?"

"A Rottweiler like Renee Duxhall."

They waited another three minutes before there was a knock on the door. Jackson opened the hatch and held up his hands as he walked out.

"Knock it off," Renee said.

Jackson grinned, knowing if Skyler's decision had been not to buy, she would have had much better ammunition.

When Tori and Kirk had filed out and taken seats, Skyler leaned forward. "One-twenty-five."

"Deal." Jackson offered his hand, and Skyler shook it. "This calls for drinks. Shane—er, Kirk, want to grab something for everybody?"

Kirk passed out lemonades and beers, then grabbed a beer for himself. Jackson hoped one wouldn't cause him to crash into the dock on the way home.

"So, cash now or cash later?" Jackson asked.

"I don't have a hundred and twenty-five thousand in cash on me at the moment," Skyler said.

"Well, where are you going to find a bank open before Monday?"

"We have a cashier's check for one-twenty-five," Renee said.

"That's bold."

"We were never offering higher."

Jackson nodded. "Let's see it."

"First the contract," Renee said.

Tori started to reach for the one she had prepared, but Renee stopped her. "I've drawn up a contract." She passed it to Tori, who spent fifteen minutes scanning the language, comparing it to the one she had forged. While she read, Jackson admired the evening colors. Eastward, the sky was still a majestic shade of blue. Beneath it, the skyline of downtown San Diego reflected the rays of the sun as it dipped toward the Pacific. The same reflection blanketed the ocean itself, coloring the water in yellows and oranges and casting distinction on each ripple and swell. It was a beautiful evening, albeit with the breeze cooling a bit.

Finally, Tori nodded. "This is good."

"You sure?" Jackson asked.

She met his gaze, her eyes confirming it before she replied. "Yes, I'm sure, Jimmy."

"All right. Then where do I sign?"

Tori passed him the contract. "It's Xed where it needs initials and a signature."

Three minutes later, Jackson had signed "James R. Dawkins" to Renee's contract. She extended her hand.

"Um, aren't we forgetting something?" he said.

Locking eyes with him, Renee opened her briefcase and withdrew a cashier's check. Jackson nodded at Tori, and Renee handed it to her.

"Is it legit?" Jackson asked.

"It's legit," Renee replied.

A moment later, Tori confirmed it. Fortunately, they had considered the possibility that Skyler would pay with a cashier's check and had researched them so she could authenticate one and so that they knew the ins and outs of cashing them. With Tori's approval, Jackson handed the contract to Renee.

"Title."

Tori passed it over.

"Keys for the engine."

Jackson reached into his pocket. "Anything else?"

Renee glanced at Skyler first. "Nope. That should be it."

"Great. You mind giving us a lift back to the dock on your new boat?"

Chapter Fourteen

Monday, May 26
10:47 a.m.

"ARE YOU SURE you have to go out today?" Hannah Douglas asked.

"I'm sure, Mom."

"You've been gone so much, lately."

"I know. I've been working. And after today, we're done."

She sighed.

"I won't be gone all day. I promise I'll be home for dinner. And catch," he added, looking over at David. "We will have a traditional Memorial Day. I just need to take care of one more thing."

"You don't want some lunch first?"

"I'm having lunch. And I'm late. I have to go."

Hannah sighed again, and Jackson gave her a kiss on the cheek. "I'll see you later. Bye, Dad."

David waved as Jackson headed for the door. Memorial Day had dawned perfectly clear after overnight thunderstorms, and the air was hot and humid. It was a perfect day for a trip to the beach.

Jackson suffered for the first five minutes on the sun-baked leather seats of the Granada. He drove with the windows down, enjoying the warm, salty breeze on his face and arms. He found a radio station that backed up Switchfoot with some Third Day, and thoroughly enjoyed his cruise to Ocean Beach. Tori and Bo were waiting outside her apartment.

She wore a white tank top and denim shorts, her hair pulled back into the stub of a ponytail. Holding Bo's leash in one hand, she had a rather traditional looking picnic basket in the other, with a towel rolled up inside the handle. Jackson got out and smiled across the car. "I'm sort of surprised you're here."

"Where would I be?"

"Considering you've got the check until tomorrow morning, I thought this might be a *The Partner* sort of deal where you didn't show up for the rendezvous." He closed his door and came around to help her with the basket.

"After all we've been through, that's all you think of me?" she asked.

"I said sort of. Hey, Bo."

"You sure you don't mind him in your car?"

"We've got a Shop-Vac." He opened the back door for Bo, then took the picnic basket from Tori. She got in, and he handed it back to her.

"How was the rest of your weekend?" Jackson asked as he got back in.

"Nerve-racking. I kept wondering where we had messed up."

"Figure it out?"

"Fingerprints on the boat."

"Hmm. We didn't touch much."

"No, but I'm sure we touched railings, walls. Left other DNA."

"Maybe the salt water will wash them away."

"Other than that . . . I think we might be in the clear."

"Here's hoping."

They headed north, across the San Diego River, and then along the coast to Mission Beach. Tori seemed to be enjoying the sea breeze as well, and they didn't talk until they arrived at the beach. Bo was eager to get out and romp around, and Tori had trouble holding onto his leash while Jackson followed with the picnic basket.

The beach was crowded, and they walked a ways back south until the crowds thinned. Tori picked a clear patch of sand, and Jackson spread out the beach towel. They sat down, and Bo, having had his fun, was content to sit beside them. But his eyes never stopped roving up and down the beach, looking for a reason to run.

"So what's in the basket?" Jackson asked.

"Ham and cheese."

"Hardly gourmet, for such a good cook."

"It was what I had on hand."

"I'll take it."

Tori doled out sandwiches, chips, and sodas while Jackson reached into the pocket of his swim trunks and pulled out a small GPS device. The last of their purchases, it had cost four hundred dollars but was well worth it in their eyes. Friday evening, Jackson had hidden a small transmitter inside the galley of *The Baby J*, behind an access panel for the refrigerator. It had enabled them to track the boat's movements. Sunday, Skyler had moved it from its slip at Shelter Cove Marina to another marina in Mission Bay, just north of the outlet of the San Diego River.

"He moving?" Tori asked.

"Not yet."

"Good thing I brought sunblock."

They ate casually, then tossed a Frisbee to Bo. After he'd had a thorough workout, they returned to the towel and some fresh-made brownies, and Jackson again checked the GPS.

"Nothing."

"Maybe they already got to him," she said. "Or maybe he changed his plans."

Jackson shrugged.

"You worried?" Tori asked.

"About?"

"Him coming after us."

"No. He has no idea who we are."

"Yeah."

"Kirk, on the other hand . . ."

"You don't have to worry about him," she said. "I talked to him yesterday. Turns out he and his dad are headed to Spain on a forty-five footer."

"Spain?"

"Derek Taylor is a world-class sailor. They're headed through the Canal and across the Atlantic."

"That will take a while."

She nodded.

"He's not running, is he?"

"They were planning on this for a while. I think they just bumped it up a little."

"Then we're good. Skyler has no idea where to start to find us, and he's going to be in too much hot water."

"You think he'll do time?"

Jackson shrugged. "He's got a good lawyer. She'll probably get him off."

Tori watched the ocean for a little while. "Another brownie?"

"You have to ask?"

She passed the container to him, and he lifted one out.

"Work's going to be kind of dull after this," she said.

"I know. It's like Hannibal always said, about being on the jazz. Coming off the jazz is hard."

"I could see myself doing this for a living."

"Yeah?"

"Yeah. I mean, I took this job because I needed work. I never thought I'd become a P.I. But after this . . . I don't know."

"You've got a knack for it. Else for undercover work. You're fast on your feet, an eye for details. And you care. That counts for something too."

Tori smiled.

Jackson ate.

"What about you?" she asked.

"I don't know. I don't think MTR's looking to add associates."

"If anything, to downsize, according to the rumors," she said. "But you could always go it on your own."

Jackson shrugged. "I don't know." He flicked on the GPS. "He's on the move."

"What?"

"Heading out of the bay."

Tori dug into the basket and retrieved a pair of high-powered binoculars. She turned them south, scanning the bay's outlet into the ocean. It ran parallel to the outlet of the San Diego River, separated by a rock jetty. Another one bordered the north edge of the bay's outlet, providing a channel for boaters.

"You got him?" Jackson asked.

"No. Not . . . Wait. I think that's him."

She passed the binoculars to Jackson, and he took a moment to locate *The Baby J*. Skyler and three others sat around the boom as Skyler charted for open water. "I think I can see a smirk from here," Jackson said.

"You want to make the call or should I?" Tori asked.

"Go for it, Walker. This was your case."

Tori retrieved one final burn phone, purchased for just this occasion. A minute later, she had patched through to an operator at the Coast Guard. "I'd like to report a stolen boat," she said. "Yes, it's a thirty-eight-foot sailboat named *The Baby J*, just taken from Marina Village in Mission Bay. . . . Allie Dawkins," she said with eyebrows raised at Jackson. When chartering the boat, he had given DP Charters Skyler's name and address, but a fictitious e-mail and number for a burn phone, expecting they would try contacting Skyler Sunday night or Monday morning when the boat wasn't returned. One of those contingencies they had thought of at the last minute. They had no idea if or when the authorities had been alerted, so she stayed in her character and hoped they didn't ask too many questions.

"Five minutes ago," she said. "It's a charter, belonging to DP Charters in Dana Point. . . . Yes, that's right. . . . Yes. . . . Thank you."

She lowered the phone, powered it off, and removed the SIM card and battery from the back.

Jackson grinned and handed the binoculars back to her. While she watched, Jackson patted Bo and had a third brownie.

"They're turning north. Perfect."

Five minutes passed. Then a Coast Guard cruiser appeared, racing north around Point Loma. Tori described the chase until both boats were clearly visible with the naked eye less than half a mile out to sea. As *The Baby J* slowed and the Coast Guard cruiser pulled alongside it, she gave Jackson a peek through the binoculars. Several others on the beach had noticed the cruiser, and Jackson heard a few murmurs as he honed in on Skyler. The binoculars were high-powered, but not enough for Jackson to make out Skyler's expression. But he was sure it was a mixture of rage, shock, and confusion. A perfect blend.

They took turns watching for almost fifteen minutes. Then Skyler and his guests were brought aboard the cruiser while one of the Coast Guard officers took control of *The Baby J*. Both vessels came around to starboard and headed south.

"And justice is served," Tori said. "I just wish I could see his face when he realizes we took him for the computers too."

"You think I'd be pushing it to call in as Pastor Chad tomorrow and tell him Pastor Cal is so taken with the Nicaraguan refugees that he's decided to stay there?"

"Maybe just a scoonch."

Jackson grinned. "Walker, I owe my pops a game of catch, but first, what do you say I buy you a double scoop ice cream cone?"

"That is a deal."

Chapter Fifteen

Sunday, August 31, 2008
8:52 a.m.

JACKSON HAD ATTEMPTED to time his arrival at Faith Baptist Church in Imperial Beach perfectly, close enough to the start of the service that a friendly elder or little old lady wouldn't start a conversation with him, but early enough to still have time to fill out his offering envelope. He was greeted warmly by a middle-aged usher with a comb-over, and found his own seat on the middle left of a moderate-sized, traditional style sanctuary. Organ on the left, pulpit in the middle, choir loft on the right. A baptismal was directly behind the pulpit, under a single, simple, wooden cross. The lighting was soft, but the room wasn't dark, and although Jackson was seated in an old-fashioned wood pew, it was padded. He wasn't uncomfortable. Then again, he hadn't sat through a forty-five-minute Baptist sermon yet either.

Faith Baptist marked Jackson's tenth church in twelve weeks. First a Catholic church in El Cajon, then a Methodist church in Emerald Hills, and after that, a non-denominational Pentecostal church in a strip mall in Rolando. He'd attended a Jewish temple and some all-encompassing "fellowship" that may or may not have worshiped Pluto. He'd sung hymns, recited the Lord's Prayer and several creeds, stopped reciting halfway through a third creed when it varied from Scripture, and heard sermons on everything from the faith of America's founding fathers to the Ten Commandments to *The Shack*. He'd been invited to come to Sunday school five times, return to church three times, and to dinner once. Twice if he counted the pastor's daughter who had hit on him at a community church in Mission Hills. Ten churches in twelve weeks had him sick of church-hopping. But this was his last one.

Jackson reached into his pocket and withdrew a standard-sized envelope. Making sure no one was watching, he retrieved thirty-four one-hundred-dollar bills and placed them in an offering envelope. He sealed it and placed it in his Bible. When the offering was taken midway through the service, he dropped it in the plate with a grin. In the last three months, Tori had visited three churches and six charitable organizations, making anonymous donations to each. With Jackson's offering deposit at Faith Baptist, they had now returned all $118,750 stolen by Chaz Skyler.

The sermon, ironically enough—and perhaps it was a sign—was about the vengeance of God. It was more of a toe-crusher, reminding the congregation that there were consequences for sin, even for the redeemed. After a closing hymn, Jackson quickly slipped out of the church. It was a great day in San Diego, and Jackson enjoyed the drive back toward his parents' home in Tierrasanta. As he drove, he reflected on the summer.

MTR Investigative Services had closed in late June due to a combination of low funds and bickering amongst the associates. Jackson had spent the summer doing temp work and odd jobs. Just recently he'd taken on a gig with a home contractor and was working fifty- and sixty-hour weeks doing everything from framing to painting. But the money was good.

Tori had taken a job with an insurance company in San Diego, and from their few conversations, was busier than Jackson. After MTR had closed, they hadn't seen much of each other. The day after Memorial Day, they had gone to Pacific View Bank and cashed Skyler's cashier's check. After plotting who would return money where, they had split the cash and gone about returning the money on their own timeline. Jackson had taken the remaining four computers, selling three of them. He kept the other for himself as a backup for his aging current laptop.

Before MTR closed, Jackson and Tori had used some of the resources there to monitor the proceedings involving Skyler. He had not gone to trial, but apparently, the incident aboard *The Baby J* on Memorial Day with potential clients and the confusion with DP Charters had caused him to lose his job at LoTek. Or maybe they had just realized what a jerk he was and canned him for their own reasons. Whatever the case, there had been no recriminations against Jackson or Tori, either from Skyler or the authorities. Jackson concluded that was half due to he and Tori being careful and smart and half due to them having been lucky.

All in all, Jackson and Tori had cleared roughly six grand after reimbursing their personal savings accounts. They'd split it and given it to the charities of their choice. Meting out justice against scum like Skyler had been enough payment, they'd both agreed. And Kirk had sent them each a postcard from Spain. He and his dad were having a splendid time, and apparently, the women of Spain were quite alluring.

David and Hannah were in Los Angeles, visiting Grant, and Jackson's absence on the trip had caused another minor tiff between the brothers. Grant argued Jackson could make his final revenge payment the next week. But Jackson had wanted to get it over with. So now he had the house to himself, and USC's season-opening victory over Virginia recorded on the DVR. He'd worked all day Saturday and hadn't had a chance to watch the game. The Trojans were loaded again, and Jackson couldn't wait to do some early-season scouting.

A red Saab 900 Turbo was parked by the curb in front of his parents' house. Jackson turned into the driveway. Tori sat on the front step, wearing the same sundress she had worn the day they sold *The Baby J*. Her hair was a little longer, a little less ruffled. Jackson got out slowly and ambled toward her.

She stood as he approached. "Hey."

"Walker. What's up?"

"I came to say goodbye."

"Goodbye?"

She nodded. "I'm moving to Las Vegas."

"Las Vegas?"

She nodded again.

Jackson shook his head. "What's in Vegas?"

"I got a job with a detective firm there. I start Wednesday."

Jackson stepped past her and sat down on the front step. She sat beside him.

"So you were serious about this P.I. business?" he asked.

Tori shrugged. "Yeah, I think so. I at least want to give it a real try. This firm said I'd have the chance to work my way up the ladder, which we really never had at MTR. So I'll see."

"I'm sure you'll do great, Walker."

She smiled. "Thanks. Anyhow, I always wanted to say thanks."

"For?"

"You know what for," she said, leaning into him with her arm. "Skyler. I couldn't have done it without you."

"My pleasure," Jackson said. "In fact, I just made the last donation this morning. Faith Baptist."

"Then our work is done."

"It is."

She looked at him for a moment, then stood. "I should be going."

Jackson smiled.

"What?"

"Nothing. I just thought this was where you'd give me the customary kiss on the cheek."

"You'd like that, wouldn't you?"

Jackson smiled. "Send me a line from Vegas. Let me know how it goes."

"I will."

"See you, Walker."

"See you, Douglas."

He watched her back to her car, waved as she got in, then headed inside to scrounge for some lunch.